LEVIATHAN

TIM CURRAN

1

Johnny Horowitz knew he was onto something when he saw the beach.

Unlike all the others on Seagull Island, this one was empty. No sunbathing tourists, no children frolicking at the edge of the surf, no teenagers swimming the currents. Not a thing, in fact. And that was the most disturbing thing about it. That was what took hold of him and held him there, would not let him go.

True, Hurricane Amelia was on its way but it would be at least a week before it even got close to Seagull. So...what then? What explained this?

It was weird.

In fact, the desertion was almost eerie.

He sat there on his rented bicycle, the hot sun of the Carolinas basking his balding head, burning the hairless flesh red. Regardless, he waited, thinking and wondering. He wasn't certain why, but this place was telling him something, speaking to him in a tongue he just couldn't quite decipher. But its meaning was all-too apparent.

Come down here, Johnny. Come see about me.

If he had been a lyre, then one of his strings had been plucked. It kept ringing out in his head.

He put the kickstand down with the heel of his battered Nike and left the winding dirt road and moved through a forest of grass down the hill. The beach was fenced off with a faded red storm fence. KEEP OUT SEAGULL ISLAND POLICE DEPARTMENT, a weathered sign said. The storm of the other night had flattened a section of it so now there was no reason to keep out.

Shit, he thought, where in the hell would I be if I listened to rules?

Nothing like authority telling you not to do something, he thought with amusement, that makes you want to do it. But it had been that way his entire life. When he was a teenager they said don't smoke and don't drink alcohol, so he smoked and got loaded every weekend. Don't do drugs, they said, and avoid premarital sex, so he toked right through high school and jumped on anything that had a hole in the bottom. And now here he was, a fortysomething man with a steadily evaporating bank account on the downward spiral of a once lucrative photography career and he was once again thumbing his nose at authority and all because of curiosity.

This is more than curiosity and you know it, he thought. This is bigger. This a gut feeling. Christ, it's practically a premonition.

He walked over the flattened section of fence and to the perimeter of the beach itself. It was incredible, really. The beaches on Seagull were crowded this time of year, three days after the Fourth of July, and here was this huge, empty expanse of white sand licked by the Atlantic.

Why the hell didn't they open this up?

Why were there no hotels around here?

He chewed his lower lip and just studied the scene. The beach extended nearly a half a mile in either direction, possibly more. It was flanked by towering, black cliffs on either side, hemmed in by the ocean and that eyesore length of fence with the signs tacked to it. It was only accessible if you were to hop the fence (or find a broken section). There was no way you could skirt the cliffs. They were sheer and deadly, the ocean battering against them with angry force. And it wouldn't be easy to land a boat: the breakers were huge and thundering as they shattered against jutting fingers of barnacled rock and subsided into swirling tidal pools. A hundred yards offshore the conflicting currents of the riptides turned the sea into a maelstrom of churning, cascading water. No, it would be suicide trying to get a boat ashore in that.

Every three-hundred feet or so there were more signs sunk into the sand.

ABSOLUTELY NO SWIMMING
STRONG UNDERTOW
SEAGULL ISLAND POLICE DEPT.

No, no conspiracy. This place was just too dangerous.

Johnny could well imagine all the swimmers that had been lost here. Once upon a time, of course, they probably even allowed sunbathing, but people in their infinite stupidity just wouldn't stay out of the water.

Yeah, that was the reason, all right...yet, what were the vibes he was getting about this place? They were strong and clear if not necessarily specific. This goddamn place was talking to him. It had a story to tell and he just had to know what it was.

He stepped out into the sand. It was like some waveless, windless sea of white broken only by rocky islands of grass and seaweed deposited by the tide. An endless expanse of alien geography. Save for the tumultuous, hammering ocean, it was silent and still and waiting. Holding its breath. And the real crazy thing was that there was not a single seagull or tern to be seen. On an island practically infested with them that was more than just a little strange.

Johnny moved along, his feet sinking in the sand, the Atlantic spray cool, the sun hot. All in all, it was just another beach. He sat down on a rock outcropping and mopped the sweat from his brow.

He was about to leave when he saw it.

About two-hundred feet from the shore, half-buried in the sand were bones.

Human bones.

The yellowed staves of a ribcage. The jutting broomstick of a femur. The jawless grin of a skull. A black sand spider casually left an eye socket and went on its way.

Johnny went on his way, too.

He went and got his camera.

2

Johnny trusted his vibes.

In his job, you got so you went on instinct and instinct alone sometimes. He worked freelance for three of the country's leading tabloids—the *Globe* was one of them—snapping photos of celebrities when they least expected it and knocking out some copy on the same. Although others considered him a member of the much-maligned paparazzi—or a "shit-crawling worm that slithered on his belly like a reptile", according to Alec Baldwin—he considered himself a photojournalist. It was his job to give people what they wanted and if that entailed digging in the dirt and crawling through shit, so be it. The checks cashed all the same.

He'd been at it for fifteen years now, ever since he got fired from the Chicago *Trib* for drinking. But that was the great thing about the freelance business: nobody gave a shit how drunk you were as long as you produced the goods. And Johnny had produced them. Like a hen putting out eggs, he filled Middle America's insatiable hunger for sleazy celebrity photos. Whether that was a disheveled Lindsay Lohan leaving a treatment center and flipping him the bird or Charlie Sheen exiting a high dollar whorehouse in a frantic cocaine rage, Paris Hilton stumbling drunk and sloppy out of a limo from a hard night of clubbing or Princess Kate sunbathing topless, the royal jewels on full display, he always brought home the goods.

He had been threatened, sued, beaten-up—Jean Claude Van Damme had once kicked him in the nuts—but like a woman's monthlies, he always returned with unsettling regularity. "Parasite? Your damn right I'm a parasite," he had been quoted as saying. "I'm a parasite feeding off the carcasses of celebrities who are sucking the blood of the general public with their questionable, over-hyped talents."

He considered one of his most redeeming qualities to be his sense of moral ambiguity. It wasn't his place to judge, only to report. He would take his photographs and write a few inflamed paragraphs, stir things up a bit as was his way, lead the viewer and reader in a certain direction and let them run wild with it. He felt no pangs of guilt over any of it and never had. He provided a saleable service. People wanted shit. He sold shit. They liked the smell and taste of it and he kept shoveling it. He was no different than McDonald's in his somewhat narrow world view. People wanted hamburgers, so they sold them hamburgers, and never once did they suffer moral pangs over the preservative-laden monkey mulch they slapped between two smoothly-engineered buns. They just counted the cash and smiled brightly. He did the same.

He was loved by his editors and loathed by nearly everyone else. But it didn't bother him. He laughed all the way to the bank. Or had, until recently. Things started to add up and his enemies grew more powerful. The lawsuits had gotten as thick as bluebottle flies on juicy turds until it wasn't just him getting sued, but the rags he worked for. He currently had six restraining orders on him (he wasn't, for example, allowed to come within 150 feet of Beyonce) and a dozen more going through the courts. The gravy train, as it were, had run out of gravy.

As Janet Baum over at the *Star* had told him, "Just back off for awhile, Johnny. Lay low, take a vacation. Celebrity memories are short. In a couple months you can come back strong as ever. Trust me, these overfed, narcissistic pukes will still be drinking and driving, still be fucking their children's au pairs, and still be snorting coke off their agent's desk two months from now. Other than posing in front of mirrors and hawking their latest tepid remake, it's what they do."

Good advice. The problem was, Johnny didn't know if he could wait two months without a goddamn check. He had a really, really bad habit of liking good booze, gourmet food, and fast cars. The payment was coming up on the Jag again and he had to make good on the timeshare in Key West. And given the state of his finances, he knew damn well that trouble was coming. Big trouble. He needed some cash and he needed it quick. Given that stalking Justin Beiber with a camera and hiding in Matt Damon's bushes was pretty much out of the question by this point, he needed to come up with something.

Janet seemed to feel that this was a golden opportunity to find himself.

Johnny laughed at that one. He wanted to find himself about as much as Cameron Diaz wanted to find pictures of her bedroom in the *Globe* that time.

No, Janet probably meant well—that was debatable—but it just proved that she did not know him. He was not about to retire or hang out a shingle and take shots of puppies and babies or open a fucking clam shack in Cocoa Beach. He was good at one thing and he knew it. When it came to dirt, Johnny Horowitz was in his element. He'd been crawling through it for years and knew it like your average earthworm.

That's why the beach was calling to him. It had a story to tell and, judging by those well-picked bones, it was one that was probably ghastly and gory and that got his blood pumping to the old levels of sheer excitement.

There was something here.

Something good.

Something *dirty*.

And nobody knew dirt better than he did.

3

"Are you saying, Sergeant, that you don't give a shit?"

"Is that what I said?"

"No, but that's what you're implying."

Costello smirked. "I'm implying nothing."

Johnny smiled and shook his head. Sometimes he wondered if all cops were thick in the head. Oh, he'd known a few good ones in his time. But it seemed that for every intelligent, sensitive, caring cop, there were a dozen Costellos: inbred, bovine, disinterested. He knew that Costello wasn't the boss here on Seagull Island. He was merely an underling with a superior named Riggs. But Riggs was on the mainland for a week, so Costello was the only game in town, like it or not.

"I'm reporting bones, Sergeant. *Human* fucking bones. Not fish bones or the remains of a value meal from Long John Silver's. I'm talking the real thing here. They're on the beach and I have this peculiar feeling they did not walk their on their own. A vein was throbbing in Costello's temple. It was big and purple. It looked like a slug trying to mate with his skull. He sighed, relaxed his hands which had bunched into fists. "Maybe we're getting off on the wrong tack here, Mister...ah...what you say yer name was?"

"Horowitz. John Horowitz."

"You don't say?"

Johnny suppressed a smile. He appreciated good sarcasm. It was an art form as far as he was concerned and he'd been practicing it since he was a snotty-nosed, mouthy little kid at St. Mathias' in Baltimore. Costello's brand was not quite his own nor was it up to his standards…yet, with that molasses-slow Southern johnnycake drawl, it had real potential.

"So you say you found bones on the beach?"

Johnny smirked himself. "I'm getting the strongest sense of déjà vu here."

"I bet you are, Mr. Horowitz. I just bet you are."

"But, yes, for the *fifth* and final time, I hope, I found bones. Human bones. You know, the kind that are inside the human body."

"I know the kind." Costello just looked at him for a moment or two. "And where did you find them at?"

"Out on the beach. The one with the fence around it."

"North Beach?"

Johnny shrugged. "If that's what you call it."

"And what in God's name were you doing out there?" Costello wanted to know. "Didn't you see the signs? It's dangerous. That beach is off limits."

"The fence was down. I just wanted to take a look."

Costello was agitated. His face was the color of broiled lobster, his eyes bulging from their sweat-greased sockets. Johnny thought for a moment that one might pop out and hit him square in the face.

"I don't know where you come from, Mister Horowitz," he said with an air of indignation, "but around here keep out means *keep out.*"

"Okay, Sergeant, don't pop a nut here. I didn't come in for a lecture about civil law, I came in to report bones. Human bones for the love of Christ."

Costello sighed and shook his huge head. "All right. All right then. Jim?" he called out.

A thin, seamed face peered into the office. "Yeah?"

"Keep an eye on things. Me and *Mister* Horowitz here," he said like he'd tasted something especially foul, "are going to take a ride."

Johnny followed his wide ass to a cruiser parked at the curb.

"Okay, Mister Horwitz. Let's see about these bones of yours."

4

Costello drove like a cop: slow, meandering.

"Seems like more people show up every summer," he told Johnny. "More people and still the town council won't loosen up the funds to put more men on. Ain't it just the way? More people. More trouble. More bullshit. But we have to get by with the same or even less."

Johnny pulled a cigarette from his pack and stuck it between his lips. "Mind if I—"

"Yes, I mind. No smoking in town vehicles."

"Sorry. I didn't take you for one of the anti-smoking Gestapo. Didn't see your party badge anywhere."

Costello grimaced. "City Council decided that. Not me. Personally, I could give a rat's ass what you put in your lungs. And the more of it, the better, I say."

"I get the feeling you don't much care for me, Sergeant."

"Where'd you get an idea like that?"

They drove in silence now that nothing was left to the imagination. Johnny had a feeling that Costello was wishing it was the good old days when he and a couple of the local boys could have taken a certain Jew boy out back and pounded some sense into him.

Like you'd be the first, he thought.

It was a beautiful warm July day. The beaches were loaded with attractive women in thong bikinis and here he was cruising the back roads with this ape. There was something terribly wrong with the picture, he decided. But as wrong as it was, it was also right because he knew he was onto something. It was not just a hunch now, it was a certainty. And the sergeant's manner had confirmed that.

At North Beach, Costello pulled over.

"Yup, fence is down just like you said."

Johnny just looked at him, choking on the sarcasm that begged to be freed.

5

Out in the sand, Johnny waited for him.

"Sure is a nice day," Costello said, lingering at the edge of the beach like a dog at the end of its chain. "Certainly is."

"Yeah, it is. Can't beat that blue sky and that white beach sand. Makes a fellow want to actually come down here and see it, close-up like."

What the fuck was with this guy?

Costello had to be nearly 6'5 and a good three hundred pounds to boot. Though he was a heavy man, he was more muscle than fat. The sort of guy who could break up fights in a biker bar single-handedly. He was big and blonde and looked hard as concrete. He could've broken Johnny in two without working up a sweat. He reminded Johnny vaguely of the stories his Lithuanian grandfather had told of the SS thugs that had brutalized Jews in the Vilna Ghetto during World War II, his family included. Yet...this homegrown cone pone Nordic warrior looked *scared.*

There was no other word for it.

This big tough cop smelled, no, *reeked* of fear.

Johnny waited there, half tempted to start kicking the bones around to see if that would get a rise out of him. Cops weren't suppose to like it when you interfered with a crime scene—if that's indeed what this was—but he had a feeling that the good sergeant wouldn't have batted an eye. He would have probably been happier if Johnny had thrown the bones right back out into the ocean.

"Are you coming down or should I carry them up to you?" Johnny asked, not withholding the sarcasm now.

Costello came down slowly, begrudgingly. "No need for smart talk, Mister Horowitz. I was simply admiring the day. There's nothing wrong with that, is there?"

Together, they moved out into the sea of sand. The sound of the pounding surf was nearly deafening. Johnny looked around and still saw no bird-life: no gulls, no terns, no pelicans, no cormorants, nothing. This beach was just as dead as the bones it had coughed up. Just as gleaming, just as white, just as inexplicably lifeless.

"Funny there's no birds around here," he said. "Don't you think? Every other beach on this island is overpopulated with them except this one. Strange."

"Not so strange. Shows common sense on their part."

"Common sense which I'm sadly lacking, you mean."

Costello shrugged his massive shoulders. "All I'm saying, Mister Horowitz, is that those signs are posted for a reason. We've lost more people...more *swimmers,* that is, on this beach than I'd care to count. And regardless of my personal feelings concerning you, I'd rather not number you among them."

"I'm touched by that, Sergeant, I truly am. But not to worry. I don't like the water and what's in it. I almost pissed my pants taking the ferry to Seagull and that is no shit. I don't even wade in inland lakes."

"Afraid of drowning, eh?"

"No, sharks."

Costello grunted.

Confessions dispensed with, they went over to look at the bones thrusting from the sand. Costello kneeled down and pulled one out carefully. It looked like an ulna. It was yellowed considerably. There was a deep gash running lengthwise. Johnny got down there now, too. Despite a certain uneasiness about touching such things, he pawed away some sand and unearthed a stout, baseball bat-like bone which he thought was a tibia. It, too, had a gash in it. That and a half-dozen smaller scratches. He'd noticed similar marks on the skull earlier when he'd returned to photograph them.

"What the hell made these?" he said, more to himself than Costello.

"Crabs."

"Crabs?" Johnny said. "Must be very big, these crabs."

"Blues," Costello told him, using a tone he generally reserved for congenital idiots. "Blue Crabs. I've seen what they do to bodies that roll in the surf awhile. Strip 'em right down. It's not pretty."

"Crabs," Johnny said again. "Well, I'll be darned."

Costello ignored him. He brushed sand away from the skull. More scratches, chips. The ribcage had them too. The sternum was nearly shattered, several ribs snapped in half.

"Lot of damage for crabs." Johnny examined the bones more closely. "Could a shark have done this?"

Costello sighed, looked out across the beach. "No...I don't think so. We don't have any big ones around here," he explained. "At least none big enough to kill someone."

"Then what?"

"Then nothing. This person probably decided to take a swim out here, maybe last season, and the riptides got 'em. The tide probably just recently spit these out. Happens."

"In which case, you must have a missing persons file on this individual."

"Can't say that I do."

Johnny chuckled. "So, when people disappear on Seagull Island you guys just shrug and go back to your grits?"

Costello stood up. He towered over Johnny. "I've about had it with your mouth."

"Okay," Johnny said. "Okay. That was probably uncalled for...but your attitude of indifference seems real suspicious to me. And before you go calling me some dumb, interfering Yankee sonofabitch...why is it you're allowing me to tramp up this crime scene?"

Costello pulled his hat off and slapped it against one meaty thigh. "First off, Mr. Horowitz,

I've never called anyone a dumb Yankee in my life. I leave that to inbred ignorant white trash that are still pissing about the damn Yankees running roughshod over great-great-great-granddaddy's hog farm. Being Southern does not necessitate being stupid. I'm an educated man. Secondly, this is not what I would call a crime scene. And even if it was, it wouldn't much matter how much we tramped about. We got high tide on this beach twice a day. Any evidence would have long been carried away. So let's not play *CSI: Seagull Island,* okay?"

"Okay."

"And as far as the identity of these bones…who can say? The county sheriff on the mainland keeps missing person's files. He might have something. Then again, he might not. This…*individual* may have fallen off a sailboat or a yacht forty miles from here. He or she could have been a hand on a foreign fishing trawler and those type of things are very rarely—if ever—reported."

Johnny smiled. Why, Costello was almost likable. He was well-spoken, apparently intelligent, and he was no fool. If it wasn't for the fact that Johnny was almost certain he was concealing something, he might have suggested heading over to the Bluefin for a cold drink.

"But these marks..."

"Probably from banging around against the rocks," Costello said with a strange rubbery smile. "Things nibbling on 'em. Maybe even sharks."

"Or crabs," Johnny said.

Again, Costello ignored him.

He seems to have an answer for everything, Johnny thought suspiciously. Maybe he was right. Maybe it was just as he said. Nothing but a swimmer, dangerous water, sharp rocks. *Crabs.* But maybe it wasn't. For reasons he wasn't quite sure of, Johnny didn't believe him.

"We better go," Costello said. "Things to do. I have to come back here with a crime scene kit and clean this up before the tourists see it and stop spending their money. A crime scene kit being your average Hefty bag in this case."

"Yeah," Johnny said. "Just watch out for the crabs."

But Costello was already across the beach, almost jogging to the hill.

6

Johnny came back again with his camera and a six-pack of Molson's on ice. He parked his bike off the road and sat on the hillside just inside the damaged fence, watching the tide come in and slugging beers. Using his telephoto, he saw very clearly that Costello had not come back with his Hefty Cinch Sak crime scene kit as promised. The bones were still there, the waves slowly rolling over them now. Within minutes, they were lost to sight. Now wasn't that something? He had been buying into what Costello said, much of it anyway, but this kind of upset the balance. Maybe it wasn't exactly a hot crime scene, but still bones were bones. They had to be collected for examination. At least…you'd think so.

Johnny sat there, working his way through his beers, troubled.

Watching the water, he thought: What sort of game are you playing at, Costello? Just what kind of shit is going on here? You can't expect me to believe you were too damn busy to come and get the bones and if you were, that someone else couldn't have picked them up for you. I get the feeling that regardless of what you said, you do think I'm a dumb Yankee sonofabitch, but on that, my friend, you are sadly mistaken. Painfully mistaken. There's something about this entire affair that doesn't wash and I'm going to find out what.

You're scared of this beach. That much is obvious. But guess what? I'm going to find out and if I learn that you're covering up something, I will spread the manure of Seagull fucking Island all over the tabloids and the internet and I will use you for a shovel. Count on it.

Still, for all his blow and bluster, Johnny did not have a clue.

There was something…but what?

It was then that he noticed a not-so subtle tingling at the back of his neck that moved down his spine and spread over the backs of his arms. It increased until he was nearly shivering with it and that made no sense because it was a perfectly warm afternoon. He could feel the heat of the day gathering around him…yet, the chill persisted. Then he noticed something else. His mouth felt almost hot. Except, it wasn't his mouth, he realized, but the fillings in his teeth—they were getting warmer and warmer. Not only that, but his gums were aching.

He stood up.

He felt weird and wobbly, waves of nausea passing through his lower belly. He wasn't sure whether he would fall down or throw up or both. Finally, white dots popping in his field of vision, he went down to his knees. His heart was pounding and the air was suddenly thick, nearly unbreathable, and hot like the tepid, humid breeze blowing out from a tropical jungle. Then that passed and the world around him was suddenly vibrant with colors. He blinked a few times and things settled down. Except for the sky…it was no longer a perfect crystal blue, but a hazy yellow blending to pink at the horizon.

What the fuck is going on here?

He had dropped his camera. His beer had spilled all over his crotch and he had not even been aware of the fact. He fumbled his cigarettes out of his shirt pocket. It took some doing to get his hand to stop shaking so he could light a butt. Finally, he did. The nicotine planed him out inside, made him feel like he was attached to the Earth again and not some helium balloon that was about to drift off into the sky.

But the world…something had happened.

The sky was still yellow. The air felt strange. Was this what happened right before a hurricane? Was Amelia closer than anyone expected? Never having been in a hurricane, he just did not know. Something was going on here; he just didn't know what. Everything else seemed the same…except for the ocean. It had been blue earlier, fading through the day to a sort of dirty gray, but now it was deep crystal green.

Hell, it's practically neon green for chrissake.

If he hadn't known better, he would have thought he was looking at a *different* ocean.

It was insane.

He brought up his digital camera and took a few shots of the water and the sky. He didn't know why, but he thought it might be important.

He pulled on his cigarette and waited.

Something was going to happen and he knew it and then it did. Off in the distance, the water started bubbling and roiling and he thought it might be the conflicting currents of the riptides reacting to the weird sea and sky, some kind of atmospheric thing. But that wasn't it at all. The water was boiling like a pot and then he saw several thrashing gray bodies out there, huge things, apparently fighting just under the surface. Then the water went red with blood and he saw a struggling form break the surf.

He was thinking whale.

He was thinking shark.

But this was neither. It looked oddly like an immense porpoise, but with the black, shiny skin of a seal. As it died, putting out a gleaming wake of blood, the thing that had delivered the death blow kept hitting it from beneath. Blood exploded, shooting up into the air in ten-foot gouts. Then a set of jaws rocketed from the maelstrom and for one brief second through the blood mist and spray and cascading water, he saw the creature's gleaming teeth...then they closed on the porpoise-thing and bit it in half quite neatly like scissors slicing a paper doll.

Johnny heard the tearing of flesh and the crunching of bones.

He could smell the meat and blood.

The stink of it made him feel almost giddy as the sea breeze pushed it into his face.

Whatever that predator was, it dove with half of the carcass, one gigantic flipper breaking the surface before disappearing. Though this all happened forty feet out in the water, he guessed that the porpoise creature was easily fifteen- to twenty-feet in length. Which made the predator an absolute sea monster.

Somewhere during all this, the cigarette had fallen from his lips and he had gone down on his knees.

He had just witnessed a sea monster attack and he hadn't even got a fucking picture.

7

Thirty minutes later, he was still there. Oh, he'd found his dignity again and planted his ass on a rock, but he was still there, his crotch drying in the breeze. He was chain-smoking and knocking back one beer after the other. A slight buzz was to be felt, but he did not feel it. He did not feel a damn thing. This was the after-effect of complete revelation— perception was narrowed and the mind was a fog of impossibility. So, he sat there, smoking and drinking. It was like his life up to that point did not exist. And when he forced himself to accept that, yes, it existed all right, it was like some absurdist comedy.

How many years now, me bucko, have you been hiding in bushes and belly-crawling through gardens and hiding under sheds to get the oh-so elusive photo of some bloated, self-important celebrity? How much time have you wasted on pedestrian bullshit like that? It seemed important, but now you know it was an absolute waste of time and don't that just hurt?

He didn't want to think about it.

He had been wasting precious time and precious thoughts on the most fleeting and ephemeral of things. He might as well have been weaving baskets or collecting bottle caps. In the final analysis, the secret lives of vain, egocentric fools like Jay Z and the Kardashians were the trivial fodder of trivial, empty minds.

There were other things to photograph.

Things beyond imagination and he had just seen a few of them.

But, revelatory as it all was, he honestly wished he had not seen it at all. It was too much. It was beyond him. The confines of his mind were too tiny to encompass something like this. So as he sat there, pulling off his cigarette (which had gone out, something he was not even aware of), he thought how very simple it would be to hop the ferry to the mainland and grab the first plane out.

But as safe and snug as that sounded, he wasn't going to do it.

He was going to stay.

Because every other spot on God's green Earth was going to seem dull and impossibly dreary after Seagull Island's North Beach.

God, he could still see those things out there.

Worse, he could smell the blood of their combat.

He tossed his cigarette away and finished his beer. He belched loudly and it actually echoed against the high towers of rock. He giggled. Then he sighed. The weird sky and ocean had faded away within minutes after the porpoise-thing died. The sky was not blue now, but more of a steel gray, threatening rain. The ocean breeze was cool. The sea was the color of fresh cement. Amelia was pushing landward. What he had seen was there and then it was gone.

How could that be?

Though he made a living taking pictures of celebrities, that did not necessitate that Johnny was a fool. He knew what he had seen. There were no whales or sea mammals or fucking sharks that looked like those things. What he had seen—and heard, and *smelled*—was a scene seventy or eighty million years gone. Yet, it had been real. For a few minutes, it had been a Mesozoic sea out there. Now how was he to make sense of that? No real world logic explained it. This was the stuff of fringe science and B-movies. He kept going through it in his mind, throwing around weighty, barely understood concepts like *time warps* and *magnetic anomalies* that really explained nothing. Something had happened. And if he was to judge by the bones and Costello's almost phobic dread of North Beach, it had probably happened before.

And would again.

"Yeah," he said under his breath. "Except next time, I'll get a fucking shot of it."

8

At the Bluefin that night, Johnny sat alone at his little corner of the bar, nursing Margaritas and thinking, thinking until it seemed like his brain would foam out of his ears. What he knew about science and paleontology and time distortions he could have carried around in a thimble. If he was going to go after this, really go after this, then he was going to need to talk with someone who knew about shit like this. But before he dared do that, he would need to know about the history of North Beach. If he went to an expert with a sea serpent story, he'd be laughed at.

He would need evidence.

Clear photographic evidence.

But I'm not here for this shit, he told himself bluntly. I came to rest, to swim, to get drunk, to pick up women. I haven't had a goddamn vacation in nearly eight years. I'm not here to figure out the mystery of North Beach or the unknown bones.

That made him smile because it reminded him of those Hardy Boy mysteries he'd read when he was a kid. They always had names like *The Secret of the Smiling Skull* or *The Mystery of Pirate's Cove.* And, with that in mind, he had a new title for the series now: *The Mystery of the Bones on the Beach.* There were also a couple companion pieces: *The Secret of the Frightened Cop* and *The Terror of North Beach.*

All of which made him think about Costello. He wasn't a bad guy as far as cops went. His job on a tourist island like this was to keep the peace and keep people safe. And so, he had done everything he could to divert Johnny's interest in North Beach. His story that the bones were all that remained of a drowned swimmer whose body had been mercilessly battered by the rocks and nibbled by crabs sounded almost logical.

But then you saw the sea monsters.

Yeah, that was it. It still didn't mean Costello was wrong. The creature Johnny had seen out there had immense crocodilian jaws. If it was responsible, it would have smashed the bones to fragments.

Granted, he thought. But Costello is still covering up something and you know it. He must be aware of what happens out there. Maybe he has even seen it. Regardless, he's fucking terrified and I honestly don't blame him.

Johnny started wondering what he might have done if one of those things had decided to come strolling out of the water like Godzilla (which seemed an apt comparison). He figured after he shit his pants, he would have screamed. And right before the monster sucked his guts out like a pimento from an olive, he would have cried for his mother.

Sighing, he drummed his fingers impotently against the bar, looking around nervously. Lovely suntanned couples everywhere. Booze flowing. Platters of seafood making the rounds. People laughing and singing along with the Jimmy Buffet tunes on the juke. It all made him ill.

This was not his scene.

"Hey, Nate?" he called out. "You got a minute?"

The bartender came over. He was dressed in a red vest and a pleated white shirt, looking very much like a bartender. His handsome black face was marred only by a white scar that ran across his forehead. The result of a marlin spike, he had admitted.

"Got more time than money, Mister—"

"Johnny."

"Right, Johnny. Keep forgetting. Now that the food's served, the drinking'll slow down for a bit. Why don't you have something? Won't find better scallops on the island."

"No, not hungry. What I need is information."

"I'm your man."

"You lived here on Seagull long?"

He smiled broadly. "Hell, yes. I've lived here my entire life. I've never even been off this rock. Never had any interest in leaving."

"Then you'd know about local happenings."

He shrugged. "When the tourists leave, there's only a handful of us left. I know all the dirt. What do you need to know?"

Johnny hesitated. This had to be worded carefully; he didn't want to sound like some nutjob, some Fox Mulder type who chased UFOs and sea serpents. He cleared his throat. "Have there ever been any shark attacks around here?"

Nate shook his head. "No, not that I can recall. Fisherman'll bring in a few hammerheads from time to time. Some spinners or blacktips. None of them are big enough to cause any trouble." He smiled. "I guess sharks do eat folks from time to time, but mostly on TV, eh? Not here on Seagull, though. Our sharks are just for show." He winked. "They like tourist dollars like the rest of us."

Johnny smiled. "Yeah, that's what I figured. Okay. How about a place called North Beach. You know of it?"

Nate shrugged. "Sure. It's fenced off, though, no one's allowed out there. Lots of swimmers have drowned in the riptides. You shouldn't go out there."

"I was out there today."

"Cops catch ya, you'll be in trouble."

Johnny grinned now himself. "I believe you. Have a lot of swimmers been lost there?"

"Yeah, I guess. It's been fenced off since I was a kid, though. I've never been out there."

"Never?"

"No, sir."

"Tell me something. Just between you and me and this bar," Johnny said with a conspiratorial gleam in his eye. "There has to be something more about that place than riptides. Is...is there a local story about the beach?"

Nate just stared at him. "Sure there is. But you won't hear any of that garbage from me. Nothing personal, you understand, Johnny. But this island thrives mainly on tourism. My employers wouldn't like it much if I were telling you horror stories and the like."

"That bad, eh?"

"Gossip mostly. Old wives tales. You know, every place has 'em. Small towns you got the local haunted house. On an island, you got a haunted beach or a cursed lighthouse. People get bored and they make up stories."

"A haunted beach? North Beach is haunted?"

"I didn't say that."

Johnny smiled again. "Okay, forget the ghosts. How about sea monsters?"

"Like I said, you won't get that nonsense from me. I have to eat, don't I?"

"All right, Nate. I read you. But is there someone around who *will* tell me? You know, a local historian, folklorist. Something like that."

Nate shook his head. "It's just a bunch of crap, Johnny. Don't waste your time. Have a drink, fill your belly, dance with a pretty girl. That's what life's about, not ghosts and monsters. Make believe stuff, that's all it is."

Johnny was not convinced because he could see something just behind Nate's eyes, sense something unsaid. It was like a sixth sense with him when things remained unspoken. "I'm going to ask you one question and I want you to answer it truthfully. What you say stays strictly between us."

Nate hesitated. "All right. As long as it does stay between us."

"It will." Johnny swallowed the rest of his drink. "Have you ever seen anything off North

Beach? Something that's not a shark or a whale? Something weird."

"No."

"You sure?"

"You said one question and I answered one question. Please, no more. You'll get me in trouble."

"All right. Then give me a name. There's gotta be someone around here that knows about this stuff. Tell me his or her name, Nate."

"I'll see if I can come up with something."

9

The thing that surprised even Johnny himself was his complete acceptance of what he had seen. There was no doubt in his mind and his usual cynicism had taken a powder. Good and fine, as far as he was concerned. In his experience, when people in books and movies ran afoul of something paranormal their first reaction was denial, then healthy skepticism followed by the usual gothic potboiler tropes that it was a hallucination or a dream or some oncoming mental disturbance. But it wasn't that way with him at all. He had seen those creatures fighting. He had seen the sky get funny and the ocean turn green. There was no denial on his part.

He believed.

But he knew others wouldn't. Maybe a few on the island would (not that they'd ever admit it), but never the world at large. And those were the people he would need to convince if he hoped to get some scientific backing on this, some expert testimony, and he damn well knew he had to have that. The wheels were already turning in his head. He was sitting on a fucking goldmine. Photos or videos of living prehistoric beasts would be priceless.

What, he wondered, would convince an expert? What would it take to get some paleontologist in his corner?

But he knew.

Hundreds of people claimed to have seen Bigfoot, but despite what the believers considered credible evidence—print castings, stray hairs, some nasty-looking scat that usually turned out to be the remains of a moose dump—the scientific establishment merely smirked and shook their heads. *You want us to believe, then bring us real physical evidence. We want a carcass. Nothing but a carcass for dissection will convince us.* Yes, yes, that was it. That's exactly how scientists thought. If they couldn't cut into something with a knife, then it could not possibly exist.

That's when Johnny started thinking about surf fishing.

10

The next three days, he went at it as Hurricane Amelia lifted up her skirts and danced a jig in the eastern sky. There were no outward signs of landfall yet on Seagull save for a few scattered showers and an angry swell to the sea. The sun was still out, the days still warm. Yet, there was something in the air and Johnny could feel it. Most of the tourists were bailing in numbers, taking the ferry back to the mainland. The streets were getting quiet. The beaches nearly deserted.

None of it slowed him down however.

There was an art form to surf casting and he was bound and determined to learn the basics. The rig itself cost him an arm and a leg, but if things went the way he hoped they would, it would be a sound investment. He went at it all day long until the high tide came back in around 7:00 PM. The guy at the fishing shop told him that he wouldn't have much luck with big sharks, anything over six feet, off Seagull but it was his time and his money. For the big boys, he said, experienced surf casters usually used a jet ski or a Zodiac raft and went out a good 500 yards or so and dropped their lines out in the deep water. The closer you got to shore, the smaller the fish would be.

Johnny wasn't about to go investing in something like that.

He had his own ideas.

Besides, he wasn't about to fool with the currents and breakers off North Beach. He went out past the bones—they were still there, though several were missing—and stepped around rock outcroppings and rotting things deposited by the tide and did some casting. He was using 100# test line with a seven foot rod and a Penn Senator reel. The first two days, until he got the hang of it, he used small pieces of ladyfish for bait, hooking them securely, then attaching the hook to a heavy duty leader and this to the line itself.

His first few hours of casting were nearly futile. He barely got the bait out twenty feet. But the more he practiced, the better he got at it…though it was still no easy bit fighting against the waves that sometimes crested up to four or five feet. Very often, his bait washed right back in within ten or fifteen minutes.

Then, purely by accident, he dropped his bait right into a subsurface current that dragged it right out into the deeps. He had over a thousand feet of line and several times he used quite a bit of it up. His catch for the first day included two clumps of seaweed, a half-eaten squid that was barely bigger than his shoe, and the remains of someone else's line, the lure of which was so rusty it must have been down there for years.

The second day was better.

He landed two small bluefish, a couple of croakers, and one respectable flounder. All of which he released back into the water after digging the hooks out with pliers. He felt pretty good about it all. He had never fished in his life and his training mainly consisted of a few articles he'd read on the internet. Not bad, he figured. Using that current, he was doing all right. The guy at the fishing shop had suggested he use a bobber being a newbie, at least until he learned how to feel for the bottom, but he also said that waves liked to grab bobbers and drag them back into shore.

Johnny didn't use bobbers.

He happily fished, standing around in his fighting harness, rod planted in the sand, and waited for the big boys while he drank beer, smoked, and ate sandwiches. It wasn't a bad way to spend the day and he really liked it. All these years he'd been missing out on this. It was hard to imagine anything quite so relaxing.

But even as he enjoyed his new pastime, he forever kept an eye on the sea and sky, waiting, always waiting for the anomaly to happen again and worrying that it never would. That what he had experienced that day was some freakish atmospheric singularity that would never happen again even if he haunted North Beach for the next hundred years.

Meanwhile, Hurricane Amelia was coming in.

His third day out there, the swells were cresting at six feet and it was getting windy, squalls of rain coming with increasing frequency. There were only a handful of tourists, but they had been replaced by groups of hurricane watchers. The ferries were only going to run one more day and the guy at the hotel said the barometric pressure was beginning to drop which hinted at heavy weather ahead. The islanders were boarding up their houses and getting ready for it.

It was also on the third day that Johnny landed several big bluefish, a couple good striped bass, and a few more flounder. Despite the weather, he was getting a handle on this and had learned to feel his way around the currents. At about five that afternoon, he took a fifteen-inch chunk of horse mullet from his cooler and cast it out, letting the currents take it into the deep water. The wind coming off the sea was throwing spray in his face and the waves were unruly and conflicting. He got a heavy strike right away and after twenty minutes of fighting, nearly landed a four-foot shark that broke the surface and swam happily away. He set up a new leader and another piece of horse mullet and went at it again.

The clouds overhead were gray, steely, piling up in high angry masses. They seemed to be blowing out seaward while a mass of jagged black clouds blew inward, intersecting them. The rain began to fall again and the sky forked with lightning. This was getting dangerous and Johnny knew it. But I'm not giving up yet, he thought, not just yet. He'd wait for the rain to get heavier and the wind wilder.

The lightning was arcing from sky to sea out there and the ocean was turbulent and gray, the high tide beginning to press in.

Grabbing his gear, he began his gradual retreat towards the hillside in the distance, playing out line as he went. That's when he noticed that the sky was getting funny again, not just stormy but weird. Out to sea, the clouds were unzipping with a peculiar pinkish seam that steadily grew darker red like fresh blood.

He felt that tingling up the back of his neck again.

Jesus.

It was happening.

It was happening again.

11

His throat went dry and the backs of his arms tingled with what felt like a discharge of static electricity. Once again, the fillings in his teeth felt hot. He was shaking all over, dizzy and disoriented, his stomach seeming to fill with grease until it felt like it was coming right up. He went down on his knees in the sand. He was burning hot, then chilled to the bone. The spit in his mouth tasted warm and sweet. His vision blurred, swam in and out of focus, then it was just like last time—the colors of the world so bright it made his head feel like it was going to fly apart.

And then—

And then it passed and he was staring out at the Mesozoic sea, so green and sparkling. A thin mist rode the waters and the air felt humid and thick. The sky above was yellow bleeding into pink. The sun blazed hot. In a moment of panic he looked behind him, hoping that he could still see the broken fence above and the road beyond it, afraid that he might be trapped in this awful place out of time.

Everything was still there.

Even the towering black cliffs and gnarled outcroppings of rock rising from the sea. None of it had changed. Only the ocean itself and the sky above the ocean were different. In fact, if he looked back towards the road, all was right. The sky was still gray and stormy, a light rain falling. The anomaly existed only out to sea. It was like a great window looking into the prehistoric world.

This time he was ready for it.

He took the digital camera out of his bag and made ready, watching, waiting. A thin mist rode the waters like steam from a pot. He saw nothing much of interest out there. No monsters thrashing in a foam of blood, just that endless expanse of green water reaching out towards continents that he would not recognize. His world and the primordial world seemed to be in some kind of sync because the tide was coming in just as it was in the "modern" world. It was gradual, but it was coming in. Already the sea was washing around his boots.

He backed up, trying to keep a distance between him and it.

The first thing he noticed was not out to sea but on the disappearing beach itself: shells, a great quantity of multicolored shells in the sand. He took a few shots of them, not knowing if they were unique to the primordial world. He took another shot of a weird looking crab crawling out into the water. There were clumps of seaweed with bugs hovering about them. The bugs looked like ordinary bugs. There was a huge clamshell, broken and half-buried in the sand. It looked interesting. He got a shot of it and some fish bones, a few scuttling horseshoe crabs. Whether they were part of this world or the other, he couldn't say.

Using the telephoto, he scanned out to sea.

In the distance, he saw five or six birds atop a shelf of rock rising from the surf that was not part of the modern world. They were odd-looking things almost like penguins, but with long necks and big beaks. They were making cawing sounds. He estimated they were four or five feet in height waddling about on ducklike feet. He got a few shots of them. As he watched, they dove one after the other into the surf.

Johnny knew without a doubt they were an extinct species.

He scanned out to sea again. The mist was heavier now…but he saw a long neck rising from the surf, then another. He photographed them. He couldn't remember what they were called, but he had seen them in museums and on the Discovery Channel: long-necked marine reptiles. Their heads didn't rise straight up like in old movies, but lifted just a few feet above the water as if they were looking for something.

Then they were gone.

Just try and deny this, he thought.

The water was washing over his boots again. He began to retreat, then he remembered his fishing rod. It was still out there, stuck in the sand. It rose from the water like the mast of a sunken ship. *Shit.* He either left it or he went and got it. He didn't spend too much time debating the wisdom of what he was doing, he waded out after it into the prehistoric sea, just waiting for some monster to seize him.

By the time he reached it, he was nearly up to his waist.

He pulled it up out of the sand as the water deepened around him. He began retreating back toward the beach as fast as he possibly could, waves covering him with spray. Something brushed against his left knee and he saw a serpentine, eel-like body swim off. He was about as scared as he'd ever been in his life.

As he stepped onto the sand, his heart banging away in his chest, he said, "Wouldn't all my celebrity friends laugh if I was gobbled up by a fucking prehistoric monster?"

There would have been a certain irony in that from his end and sheer poetic justice on theirs.

He got about three feet into the sand when something yanked on the line which was still out in the depths. It nearly pulled him off his feet. *You got one.* He was tempted to cut the line, but he had no intention. If he could land something, anything, it would be priceless and he knew it. The carcass of a prehistoric animal, even a small one, would be worth millions.

Calming himself, breathing in and out slowly, he went through the drill. He marched far up the beach, his quarry tugging at the line. When he was about twenty feet from the water's edge, it ran, yanking the line taut and pulling him right over, actually dragging him through the sand for three feet.

This is one tough little monkey, Johnny thought.

He was beyond being nervous by that point; he was nearly hysterical with it. Exhilarated, breathless, but mostly terrified at what might be at the end of the line. He was afraid it would break and he would never land his trophy beast. But maybe that would be for the best. Then he could make a hasty retreat back to the Blue Fin for clams and booze.

Bullshit. You're not turning back now.

"Play it out," he said under his breath. "Give and take."

He locked the reel down, playing his trophy. When it pulled back, he gave it room. When the line slackened, he pulled. This went on and off for maybe twenty minutes until he was so exhausted he was ready to pull his knife and slice the line. After all, he was an amateur. Who was he to land something like this, whatever it was? A pro fisherman would have had his hands full with a beast out of the Mesozoic.

But his trophy was tiring.

He could almost feel it. It wasn't pulling back so hard now. Each time the line went slack, he was reeling more and more of it in. Nervous, shaking, he kept tugging and reeling, tugging and reeling. And then—

And then it was in the shallows, right at the edge of the water and he saw it quite plainly. It was like an illustration from a book on fossil life. The first thing his eyes took in was a cone, what appeared to be a six foot cone that was ribbed and shiny and almost iridescent. It caught the prehistoric sun, glittering and gleaming. Then he saw the beast itself—blood red, writhing, a primitive squid with squirming tentacles, the majority of its body tucked into the cone like a nautilus in its shell. The cone was long and tapering like a dunce cap, narrowing to a tip that looked sharp.

Johnny could see the lethal beaklike mouth ringed by tentacles. It was an instrument designed by nature to tear, gouge, and crush.

But what disturbed him most were its eyes.

They were flat yellow and unpleasantly human-looking. They seemed to be looking right at him with a hatred that was nearly indescribable.

Its tentacles toyed with the line as if it was trying to figure it out.

Maybe it was.

"Get that picture," Johnny said under his breath.

He got the digital out. The squid was about fifteen feet away and he had no earthly intention of getting any closer. His hands were shaking so badly that he nearly fumbled the camera and dropped it into the sand. He brought it up to his eye and the squid seemed to flinch in much the same manner as celebrities did when Johnny leaped out of the bushes at them, camera in hand. He was struck by the most unnerving feeling that the squid was not unaware, that it was not some stupid beast, but a cunning thing.

He took three shots, then several telephoto close-ups of its tentacles, its cone, and those angry eyes that put a chill right up his spine. Satisfied, he tucked the camera back into his waterproof bag.

"Now what?" he said.

But he knew what he had to do. He'd brought that ugly cuttlefish in this far, now he had to land him the rest of the way, drag him up higher into the sand and asphyxiate him. He—or she—couldn't possibly live out of the water for very long.

In the back of his head, Johnny was already counting the money this horror would bring.

He started dragging it out of the surf as the tide advanced, waves breaking over its cone. He got the squid maybe five feet onto the dry sand when it went positively wild. Its tentacles were flailing like threshing hooks. It yanked on the line and then neatly cut it with its beak. Then it jetted itself back into the surf with amazing speed, expelling water from its spout. Its cone was rocketlike and streamlined, cutting right through the waters like a torpedo.

Then it was just gone.

But I got you, Johnny thought. Oh yes, I do.

He stepped away from the prehistoric sea, climbing the sand hills up to the broken fence with his gear. Rain was falling, a low wind moaning in the distance. Far out to sea, he saw a huge head rise up on a graceful neck and then disappear.

And as he watched, whatever atmospheric anomaly opened the passage to the prehistoric world, promptly closed.

12

When he got to his hotel room about an hour later, there was a message on his machine from Nate. He had tracked down the name of a local historian and folklorist and where he could be found. The message ended with Nate saying, *"Remember now: just between you and I. Tell no one about this. Leave my name out."* And Johnny laughed at that, laughed as he lowered his aching body onto the bed. Have no fear, Nate old boy, you are a confidential informant and I never reveal my sources. You can count on me to leave your name out of things just like you can count on me not to share the success and money this is going to bring.

Yes, this was working out good.

His little vacation from life was turning into a cash cow and he was going to milk that bitch until she bled.

13

It was early the next morning when he made it out to the end of Rocky Cape. It was a three mile journey from the town proper, about a half a mile from North Beach, so he rented a little Ford Fiesta instead of biking it out there and showing up on the doorstep panting and dripping wet.

He saw the houses right away. They were all small and practical, some of them up on stilts. They were clustered together at the edge of the sea. Several long piers ran straight out into the ocean, trawlers and skiffs moored to them, immense trawl nets drying in the sun. There were fish huts and weathered gray clapboard structures built right on the docks, wooden planks taking the places of steps leading up to the doors. Most of them looked long abandoned, leaning out over the water, windowless and ruined. Ancient waterlogged pilings marched out into the depths beyond. It was a grim and austere scene like something from a Winslow Homer painting, a commentary of man's epic struggle trying to wring a living from the angry sea.

Rising up in the gloom and casting its shadow over the houses was a large three-story building bleached by the salt spray. Faded lettering claimed that it had once housed the Atlantic Canning Company...but that must have been many decades ago. The building was dirty and decrepit, windows boarded over, gulls perched on the warped roof, great holes eaten in the walls. It was a crumbling relic from the days before factory ships. It looked like an artist's impression of a haunted house.

According to the map, this dying little community had once been called Seal City, a fishing village of sorts, now it looked half-deserted, ruined, more like Lovecraft's Innsmouth than Steinbeck's Cannery Row.

Johnny spoke with a few fishermen and they pointed him to Matt Packard's place.

It sat away from the others and away from the docks, right out on the exposed rocks of the headland, a trim white cottage. Prey to wind and weather and turbulent sea. It had a fine view of the small cays stretching out into the Atlantic like rocky fingers. On the farthest cay there was a lighthouse rising like a spire in defiance of the thrashing surf. The tourist map told him it was called the Bristol Point Light or Old Bristly. It was automated. But as Johnny looked at it out there with tongues of mist swirling at its base, he just couldn't help but imagine some grizzled old lightkeeper ascending the spiral stairs with a pegleg.

He walked up the sandy path and prepared to pound on the door.

"What the hell do you want here?" a gravely voice asked.

Johnny looked around. Then he saw a face pressed to a screened window off to his left.

"You're on my property, mister. I ask you again: What the hell do you want?"

"Mister Packard? My name's Johnny Horowitz. I have a few questions about local...ah...history. I was told you might help me."

"Who the hell told you that?"

"A guy in town."

There was silence for a time. Then: "Bring any booze?"

"No. No, I didn't."

He sighed. "Door's open."

Johnny went in and almost fell over Matt Packard.

The old man—and he *was* old, his hair frosted a snowy white, his wide face showing more wrinkles than an unmade bed—was in a wheelchair. He had his legs tucked under a blanket, but they looked wasted and thin like dehydrated saplings. He wore a faded blue workshirt, his massive forearms great slabs of meat.

"Johnny, you say?" he asked and it seemed more a command than anything. Johnny nodded.

"That's a good name. I've known a few and they always did right by me."

Johnny nearly blushed. It was apparent that old Matt Packard had never known one called Horowitz.

"I'm always happy to share history, chief, always happy. Don't get many visitors and the ones that I do seem preoccupied with getting me into a nursing home," Packard lamented. "You ain't one of those, are you, chief? No, you ain't. I can see that. But you do bother me all the same. Sure as shit."

Johnny stood there, feeling awkward. "How so?"

"In my day when you went to visit people and ask their help, you always brought beer. Sometimes a bottle. But that's okay, chief. Next time maybe." He winked at Johnny and sighed. "Just as long as you understand right now that you ain't getting none of my beer. Not that I'm unfriendly, mind you, but it ain't so easy getting my own account of the chair."

Johnny made a mental note to drop a few cases off. Maybe a bottle of good brandy, too.

The old man led him through his cluttered little house into what might have been a den but looked more like a newspaper archive. There were shelves and tables literally inundated in books, magazines, and newspapers. Place smelled like a public library. Like the rest of the house, most everything was set down low where a guy in a wheelchair could get at it.

"Have a seat, chief," Packard said. "If you can find one."

Johnny unloaded books off an old easy chair and sat down on the torn cushions. The chair swallowed him like quicksand, his knees suddenly at eye level.

There were paintings on the walls, old prints mostly. Barks and brigs and whaleboats battling violent seas. One showed a massive white whale staving in the hull of a big four-master. Above the fireplace was a lithograph of some huge octopus or giant squid tearing apart a sailing ship. Its massive tentacles were coiled like serpents around the masts and rigging, turning the vessel to matchwood.

Maybe this guy is the one, he thought. He seems to be into weird shit.

"You like my pictures, chief?" Packard asked.

Johnny told him that he did.

"Sea monster one is pretty interesting. Look at the size of that thing."

Packard grunted a laugh. "Ain't no sea monster, chief. Giant squid."

"That big?"

"Some say so. Why I knew a fellow once who said...*well,* you didn't come here to listen to my sea stories, now did you? Maybe another time. Just what did you come for?"

Johnny couldn't help looking at his legs, wondering.

"Shipwreck, off the west end, chief. No, I don't mind. Reef tore her up into kindling. I clung to a piece of the wheelhouse, but the waves smashed me into the rocks one too many times. Hurt my spine. Been in this chair since," he explained without emotion. "But I was the lucky one. I lived. Everyone else went to the bottom. Including my kid brother."

"I'm sorry."

"Don't be. Thirty-five years ago. Not worth discussing."

Johnny broke in before he digressed yet again and told him what he wanted to know. He wanted anything on North Beach. He had to go slow here, so he left out the idea of sea monsters and time gates and went after the bones that Costello seemed to have no interest in.

"Donny Costello ain't a bad sort," Packard began. "He really ain't. I shipped with his old man a few times. Like the kid he wasn't too bright, but honest and dependable."

"So what's got him spooked?"

"That goddamn beach. Lot of people here are spooked by it."

"I get that impression. I can't say it's not weird…I had a funny feeling while I was there," Johnny said, spreading the manure. "But what are we really talking about here? Not ghosts or anything like that."

"No…not ghosts. Not exactly. Other things. Flesh-and-blood things."

"What do you mean? Like monsters?"

Packard narrowed his eyes. "Call it what you want. Things happen there and things are seen there. Let's leave it that."

But Johnny wasn't about to do that. "What sort of things?"

"Creatures," he said. "Things that don't belong. A fellow like you might call them sea monsters."

"Sea monsters?"

Packard's seamed old face was set stiffly. It was no joke; his wasn't the face of a man who'd gotten off a good one. He *knew.* He knew exactly what was going on there. "Like I said, chief, I'm more than happy for the company…but if you came here to laugh at me, you'd best turn your sorry ass around and get the fuck out."

Johnny sat there. "I saw one," he said.

Packard was looking at him now. "Did you?"

"Yes."

He had the suspicion from the very first that Packard wasn't buying his supposed interest in local history. The old man was not stupid. People his age had an almost sixth sense and a highly-attuned bullshit meter. Johnny knew that if he wanted to know what Packard knew, he'd have to give him something, show his hand. That's how it worked. You show me yours, I'll show you mine.

Without further ado, he pulled out the digital camera. "This is going to sound crazy, but…" He marched right into it: the sky, the weird atmospheric stuff, the prehistoric ocean. Then he showed the old man the pictures of the squid, the birds, the long-necked things in misty sea.

"Good stuff," Packard said. "Very good. Those birds are *hesperornis,* flightless birds. They dove into the sea for fish. They stood almost as tall as you or I…you in this case. Looks like you got a few camera-shy plesiosaurs there…and that squid here is a *baculite,* a type of ammonite that went the way of the dodo bird and the moa during the Cretaceous extinction event. Too bad you couldn't have brought him in. Paleontologists would be shitting their pants."

Packard did not say anything for a long time after that. Finally, he had Johnny get him a beer and even told him to help himself. "So you know," he said. "You know about the Gateway."

"Gateway?"

"Yes, son, that's what it is—a Cretaceous Gateway. It opens time and again and very few outsiders have ever been there when it does."

The old man told him that it happened regularly when a hurricane was brewing. It had something to do with the electrical field of the storm itself and the magnetic disturbances it caused. That was the only thing he could figure. Some weird geomagnetic thing that opened the Gateway. When that happened, the sky got funny and the sea changed and the old world intersected the new.

"It doesn't occur often," Packard told him, "except when you got a hurricane or a powerful tropical storm brewing. That's when things tend to happen. You come back next winter, chances are you won't see anything out there. You could wait months for something to happen."

"Has anyone ever come here to study it?"

Packard chuckled. "Of course not. Those islanders that even know about it would never admit to such a thing out loud. Hell, they wouldn't even admit it to themselves."

"But that's insane. Something like this…hell, it would set the scientific world on its ear."

"Maybe. First off, if I know my scientists—and believe it or not, I have known a few—you'll have the devil of a time getting them to believe you and invest their time in something like a time gate. They'd dismiss you as a crackpot. Even if they suspected you were onto something, no way in hell they would risk their precious reputations with something out of the Twilight Zone like this. Sad but true. The days of the great thinkers and scientific adventurers are long gone. There's no Darwins or Curies or Einsteins left. Rest of 'em are too worried they won't get their three-year grants to study penguin snot in Antarctica or the urine flow of the Lesser Cockgobbler."

Johnny laughed. He liked this guy. He really, honestly liked him.

"You laugh, son, but it's a tragedy. The great scientific thinkers are a vanished breed. Now they're all suits and corporate fuck-wanglers playing grab-ass and sniff-the-wallet. They wouldn't have the balls to put it on the line with real world-changers like evolution or nuclear fission or even the Big Bang itself. Flat-Earth science is all the rage."

Johnny figured he was right. The real big theories and advancements in science came from people who were so obsessed with the truth that they were willing to risk everything to prove it. Some succeeded, some failed—at least, initially— but they were in there pitching, knowing that they were onto something and nobody, *nobody,* was going to convince them otherwise.

"It's a money matter here," Packard said, slowly sighing. "This place has been a tourist trap for decades. Christ, going right back to the 1950s at least. People here? Oh no, they wouldn't take a chance with that. They make their money for the whole year during the in-season."

Johnny pulled out a cigarette. "You mind?"

"Not at all."

"But that just shows how fucking stupid these people are…no offense…"

"None taken."

"…this…this is a goddamn gold mine, Matt. You know it, I know it. Sure, maybe that thing only opens now and again when the atmospheric conditions are right, but do you have any idea what people would pay to see something like that? Goddamn, every man, woman, and child on Seagull could be driving a Porsche. Hell, I fished that prehistoric sea…that squid is like nothing on this Earth. Something like that must have died out twenty million years ago."

Packard chuckled. *"Sixty-five* million years ago, chief. What you seen out on North Beach was the late Cretaceous Period, I believe. It closed sixty-five million years ago with the mass extinction of the dinosaurs and the great sea reptiles. Some three-quarters of the species on Earth were killed off. It's known as the K-T Extinction, the Cretaceous-Tertiary Extinction. The K-T Boundary marks the end of the Mesozoic Era and the beginning of the Cenzoic. Most think it was that goddamn monster of an asteroid that smacked into the Yucatan Peninsula down in Mexico. Maybe multiple impacts. Regardless, it happened and that world died out. Its story exists only in the rocks now…unless you happen to be on the North Beach of Seagull Island at the right time on the right day."

Johnny was impressed.

Packard was no old, eccentric coot. He knew his science. He had no doubt made a study of North Beach phenomena.

"Rich men would pay real money to cast their lines into the Cretaceous sea, Matt," he said.

"Oh yes. Just try to get the idiots around here to see that." Packard pulled on his beer. "They live in fear of that beach. At least, the older ones do. It's like some tribal taboo with them. They won't go out there and they won't talk about it and most claim they don't believe the old stories."

Johnny sipped his beer and pulled on his cigarette. "I'd like to hear those stories."

"Would you?"

"Yes."

"It would take hours to recount them all. Instead, I'll tell you one story. This one is better than the others because I was there. I can tell you exactly what happened. Sixteen people died. Know that, chief. It was an awful affair, but I'll tell you because I haven't talked about it in years and I'd like somebody to know what really happened that day. Jeb Connelly passed of a stroke fifteen years ago and as far as I know, he was the last survivor of that affair other than myself."

Johnny pulled out a little digital voice recorder. "You mind if I record this?"

"Nope. I'm getting on in years. This'll probably be the last time I ever tell this story so at least there'll be a record."

14

It was July of 1937, chief, and by God, I sound like an old fart, but I do remember it well. It was my twelfth birthday and my mom got some fool idea about having this big party for me. And guess where she wanted to throw it?

Well, I can see you already guessed that much.

Down on North Beach it was. She invited half the Packard clan and half her own people—the Talbots. It was quite a shindig and there had to be forty or fifty assorted men, women, and children there. Even my cousin Roy showed. He'd lost an arm to the Hun in France. After the war, well, he was still a young man, but without his hook, he wasn't much good for anything but drinking. But on that day, even he was sober. I'll never figure out how my old maw put it all together, we being so damn dirt poor and it being the depression and all, the cannery barely operating. But she had her ways as I suppose most do. I'd never seen so much food and so goddamn many presents. They ranged from something the size of a washing machine from my Uncle Alonzo to little bitty things wrapped in newspapers from my sisters.

It was something, all right.

As I recall it was a warm day. Sky blue and cloudless. You couldn't have asked for more. There were badminton nets set up and the girls were all in their bathing suits. Oh, those suits didn't show skin like they do today, but you still got an eyeful of leg and bare shoulder, maybe some belly or cleavage if it was a more risky suit they was wearing. And when you're twelve, chief, and you're starting to feel the stirrings of what it is to be a man...well, you get the idea. I was happier than I've ever been since.

Anyway, about one or so me and my kid brother Joey and Albert Johansen, my best friend, were scooting around up near the road. And that's when it happened. Albert asked me if I heard something. I hadn't but Joey did. A rumbling, he said. We all looked up, expecting to see some thunderheads blowing in from the sea, but that's not what we saw at all. You know what we saw, chief, having seen it yourself. The sky got all funny, kind of yellow going to pink and red as blood at the horizon. It was weird and kind of scary because the breeze had been blowing and suddenly everything was still. I remember looking down and seeing that everyone at my party was kind of frozen. They were locked down and still like insects trapped in amber, all of them looking up at the sky. We'd been having some weird electrical storms off and on for weeks, so I guess, looking back, I'm not all that surprised by what happened that day.

The air got real funny, hard to breathe...it was like trying to suck a breath through a hot washcloth as I recall. Down on the beach, people were dropping into the sand, shaking and vomiting. Marion Weeden, my next door neighbor, had gone into some kind of convulsions. Then, just as quick as it had come, all that passed and the sea was pea green, the breakers high—much higher than they had been before. A heavy mist was blowing in, tangling around peoples' legs, and it looked like everyone down there was standing in a white pool. I think they all knew something very strange had happened, but most didn't know what. Those that did grabbed their kids and hightailed it up to the road and got the hell out of there.

But most stayed.

That's what I remember, most stayed.

"What the heck is going on?" I remember Joey saying. "Matt, what the heck is going on?"

But I didn't know. I didn't know a damn thing. I just stood there next to Albert, stiff as a post.

People started to scream down on the beach. They were running around, panicking like ants when you step on their mound. I remember my little twin cousins calling for their mama and grown men crying out like babies. And my mom's face...oh sweet Jesus...my mother's face just white as flour. The badminton nets spilled over and so did the tables full of presents and food and drinks. My cake flipped into the sand. The ground—the beach, I mean—was *moving.*

It felt like an earthquake...except it was not a long rolling seismic sort of wave, but more of a *boom, boom, boom* like in that old picture where Godzilla comes ashore. *Boom, boom, boom.* The mist had gotten so thick you could no longer see the ocean. Hell, most of the beach was disappearing fast in that blowing white fog. I remember Joey grabbing my arm. I remember Albert holding onto me. The three of us wanted to go down there and help, but we were welded together. We couldn't move. We just couldn't goddamn move.

That quake kept rolling. We couldn't feel too much of it up on the road, but down on the beach it was plenty bad. The sand was shaking and people were falling on their asses and shouting and demanding to know what the fuck was going on. And through it all, that *boom, boom, boom* getting closer and closer. Joey was crying by then and I think I might have been, too. I remember Albert and I looking at each other as if we were goading each other to move, to go down there, to help out…but we did not move. We were kids, chief. Just goddamn kids and we were scared white.

Then we smelled something. How do I describe it to you? It was the stink of a thousand dead fish thrown up on a thousand beaches, bloating hot and maggoty in the sun. That was it, only worse. The stink of a trawler's nets and a fish cannery bleeding rivers of guts and scales and slime…a black smell, chief, just as dirty and obscene as you can imagine. Joey went right down to his knees and I clearly remember gagging, my guts filled with warm chum.

What we were smelling, you see, was the thing coming out of the sea. The thing whose mighty tread made the ground shake—*boom, boom, boom.* The thing whose slaughterhouse stench was blowing hot and wet right into our faces. We saw it about then. Just about the time those booming footfalls were so loud I had to cover my ears. The three of us saw it and, God help me, I never want to see something like that again. The mists parted and we saw a long neck rising up forty feet with a crocodile-like head on top of it that looked big as a delivery truck. The creature pushed up farther onto the beach and those poor people down there….*Jesus*…I don't think they saw it until it was right on top of them, towering over them with a tooth-filled mouth on that long sinuous python neck.

Joey screamed.

Albert ran.

A few others took off with him.

I stood there, unable to move. I shook and drooled and pissed my pants, but I could not have moved had that thing been about to step on me. It moved out of the deep sea-mist, but it was still caught in the haze of it. As it came forward, making the earth shake, its head moved side to side like that of a crawling snake. Sometime around then, its mouth yawned open like it wanted to swallow the world and I'm not the one to say that it couldn't have. The mouth, way up high above the people scrambling and lost in the fog of the beach, opened wide and the beast roared with a low baying sort of sound that was so damn loud I heard a ship far out to sea answer it with three shrillings of its fog whistle.

That's the best I can describe what I saw. What came next is the thing that made me drop senseless into sand. That long neck arched and the mouth, wide and toothed, swept about, snatching up people and eating them whole. I clearly remember the sound of crunching bone, the screams, and the sight of that monstrous yellow-eyed head with its train tunnel of a mouth seizing people and eating them, swallowing some of them and biting others right in half. Those it didn't eat, it smashed to sauce with its immense feet or crushed with its swinging tail.

That's the story. That's what I saw. That was my twelfth birthday party. That was a goddamn long time ago and a lot of people died that day including my mother. I spent a lot of time trying to convince myself it never happened, but it happened, chief, oh yes, it certainly did. Some years back before I lost use of my legs, I was invited to my great niece's birthday party. It was a theme party, as people will do these days. The theme was dinosaurs. I never went. The last thing I wanted after my twelfth year was to go to a fucking birthday party with a dinosaur.

15

Packard finished his beer. "That's it, that's the works. That's my story. I turned twelve, I lost my mother and a lot of friends, and I saw a sea monster…all on the same goddamn day. How do you like them apples?"

"A dinosaur," Johnny said, as if it was a new word or one he had never really contemplated before. "A fucking dinosaur."

"Not really, chief. You see, dinosaurs lived on land. What I saw was a marine reptile, a Cretaceous marine reptile. But…what's in a name? I saw it. Lots of us saw it, but very few of us ever talked about it."

"What happened? What was the aftermath?"

Packard thought about it a moment as he'd probably been thinking about it the past seventy-odd years. "The thing killed everyone…then it went back out into the sea. Ten minutes later, the sky was normal and so was the ocean. They never found any remains, or so they said. I think a few days later they found a shoe or something. A shoe, chief. A child's fucking shoe." He shook his head. "When Joey and me and Albert told 'em what we saw, they told us we were crazy, more or less. The authorities back then came up with a better story: a freak wave. It came up, crashed into everyone, and sucked them back out into the depths. Albert told me later that he heard there were big footprints down there and that the sheriff photographed them. If that's the case, Donny Costello might very well have them in his files to this day, under lock and key. No matter. It was swept under the rug. The three of us saw what we saw. Shortly afterwards, that beach, that goddamned cemetery, was fenced off. Been like that since. And now you know the story, chief. Joey died in the same wreck that took my legs and Albert...Albert died fighting the Japs on Tarawa."

"But other people saw it."

"Most of them had hightailed it out of there by then. They knew something was coming and they weren't too interested in seeing what it was. Not that I blame them anymore than I blame myself. I still wonder if I had moved my ass and got down there if I could have saved some of them. Especially my mom. Oh, hell, she was the tops, she was one swell lady. I wish you could have known her."

Johnny didn't ask any questions for a few minutes after that. Packard's eyes had gone misty at the memory of his mother. He was not about to disturb that. When he did speak, he said, "There was nothing you could have done, Matt. No man or boy was up to tangling with that thing."

"Sure, sure, I know. I tell myself that every day. Sometimes I almost believe it."

He told Johnny that Seagull Island had a history of sea monster sightings that went back centuries. "The Cherokees used to paddle out here to dig clams, chief, but they didn't go to North Beach. They knew. Just like the first settlers here knew. One old injun told me that the Cherokees used to dispose of their criminals and outcasts by dumping them on Seagull…when the conditions were favorable, if you know what I mean."

"Is there anything else?"

"Lots, chief, lots. But I'm old and I'm tired and I don't feel much like recounting sea monster stories to you or strange carcasses that have washed up on beaches. But I will tell you this. I mentioned Jeb Connelly. He used to date my sister. He was ten years older than me. Well, he called newspapers in Wilmington and Jacksonville, even far away as Raleigh, trying to get them to take interest in what had happened. They pretty much all dismissed him as a crank. The only reporter that showed was some drunk that came down from Norfolk. He picked up the story, all right, and the *Virginian-Pilot* ran it…but, as you might suspect, it was a humor piece poking fun at the hayseeds of Seagull Island and their quaint beliefs. Well, I don't think *hayseeds* was the word used, something possibly more derogatory like *clam-diggers,* I believe. How they found humor in sixteen people missing is beyond me."

"That's quite a story," Johnny said. "If I hadn't seen what I've seen I probably wouldn't believe it."

"Wouldn't blame you," Packard said. "It happened, that's all I can say…but, then again, folks here on the island do say I'm a crazy old man."

16

By the time Johnny got to the Bluefin that afternoon, he had a headache.

He sucked down Bloody Marys and ate steamed shrimp and oysters, thinking and thinking and thinking. He had pictures, but he would have liked a specimen. Pictures could be faked…though, as he sat there looking at them, he had to admit they looked pretty damn good. Clear for the most part, but certainly not professional by any means. His experience with monster photos was that they were either too fuzzy to make out or so expertly done that they were suspect.

Not mine, he thought. These are good. Enough to make even one of Matt Packard's flat earth scientists pause and take notice.

After he'd been there about an hour, Nate came on. He kept giving Johnny little sidelong glances. Finally, Johnny called him over. "Refresh that," he said, handing him his glass. "And thanks for the top secret info on Matt Packard."

"You went to see him?"

"Oh yes."

"And?"

"He's interesting."

"He's a nice fellow, but he does like to tell tall tales."

"He might like to spin a few," Johnny said, "but that doesn't make him a liar."

Nate went off to refresh his drink. He took his time coming back and probably because he knew he was going to get pelted with questions. When he set the drink down, he tried to make a hasty retreat but Johnny wasn't having that; he started pelting him.

"Tell me, Nate. Have you heard any of Matt Packard's stories?"

"Oh, a few."

"And?"

"Ah," he said, laughing and dismissing it all with a wave of his hand. "It's nothing. He just likes to talk."

"So you don't believe what he says about North Beach?"

Nate looked uncomfortable. "It's all before my time. What would I know of that?"

"Have you ever seen one of them."

"What?"

"You know what."

Nate sighed. "No, Johnny, I haven't. My mother was a wise woman and she told me never to go out to North Beach and I never have. Now, enough of that. You need to start making plans, my friend. The ferries aren't going to be running that much longer. We're closing up shop here tomorrow. You might want to get off the island before the real bad weather starts."

"I'll keep it in mind."

"You do that, my friend. Barometric pressure is starting to drop. That's not so good. You don't want to be here when the storm hits."

But he was wrong on that—this is exactly where Johnny wanted to be.

17

After he was well fed, had a good buzz going, and took a little nap, he went out on the terrace of his hotel room and watched the angry gray clouds moving in the sky. He had a cigarette and called Janet Baum over at the *Star*. He had to start the ball rolling on this and she was always a good place to start.

"Well, if it isn't the esteemed Johnny Horowitz," she said. "How goes things? Getting your fill of sun and fun? Eating well? Drinking well? Sunbathing? Helping tanned young ladies out of their thongs?"

Johnny told her he was doing most of that, but staying away from the girls.

"Since when do you stay away from women half your age?"

"Since I found something more interesting."

"Oooo, Johnny. You've come out at last."

Typical Janet. "I have a question for you, dear. How much, do you suppose, a shot of a real live, breathing sea monster might be worth?"

There was silence on the line. He couldn't have shut her cheeky mouth much quicker had he shoved a hand towel in there. She did not speak for some time. He heard her breathing and finally she cleared her throat. "Are you drinking?"

"Yes, of course I'm drinking, but that's beside the point."

"Johnny…dear God, you're serious, aren't you?"

"I've never been more serious."

"Well…um…that is…I mean if there was such a thing as a sea monster—"

"Oh, there is, darling. You only have to know where to look."

"—then, well, I suppose such a picture would be worth quite a bit." She cleared her throat again. "Johnny, please tell me you're not fucking with me. I'm just not up to it, okay? Bob left me and I'm a complete wreck."

Bob was her cat. "He's left before. He's chasing tail. When he's had his fill, he'll come back hungry and tired."

"Do you really think so?"

"Of course, Janet. Just relax. Bob is Bob. You know what a whore he is."

"I suppose you're right."

"But to answer your question, no, I'm not fucking with you. I've seen shit here that makes me think I've wasted my life taking pictures of Hollywood gutter puppies and suckmongers. I'm serious. I'm absolutely fucking serious. If you don't believe that, check your email and check it right now."

Janet did. He could hear her clicking away. She giggled. "Johnny…is this your penis?"

"Delete that one. I was experimenting with the camera."

"Naughty thing." He heard her clicking away. She started making sounds and he knew she was more than a little impressed. "This is…this is fucking weird, Johnny. Those birds. I have to admit I've never seen birds like that and those necks out in the water…well, they look pretty authentic. A lot of this other stuff, I can't say. But…*gah*…that squid, now that's certainly nasty. I've never seen one with a cone shell like that except…oh my God, *yes,* I have. That thing is a prehistoric animal, isn't it? But it's not a fossil…"

"Does it look like a fossil? I caught it on hook and line surf casting with shark bait. And it wasn't too fucking happy about it either."

Janet was silent for a time and he could imagine her perusing the photos. "Johnny…just where the hell are you staying? Jurassic fucking Park?"

"About as close to it as you can get without a time machine, dear."

"Okay, okay. Now tell me how this works?"

This was the thing he absolutely did not want to tell her about, but he did. "That's all I can tell you. Everyone here is afraid of that beach and I can see why. It has a history of sea monster sightings and weird animals washing up on the beaches. It's some kind of time anomaly. The guy I told you about claims it's a Cretaceous Gateway. It's more than a window into the Cretaceous, it's a fucking doorway. It's unbelievable."

More silence. "You have no idea how badly I want to laugh at you," Janet said, "but I can't laugh at these shots. Would you mind if I showed them to someone? Just a friend who happens to be a paleobiologist at the Smithsonian. If this shit is real, she'll know it."

"I suppose that would be all right."

"I'll give her your cell number. She might want to talk to you."

"That's fine."

"Johnny...that hurricane is getting close. Do you think you should get out of there?"

"No, if what Matt Packard said is true, the electrical and magnetic fields of good old Amelia are going to kick the Cretaceous door wide and I'm going to be there when it happens with film in my camera."

After he hung up, he stood there staring out at the raging sea. The ball was rolling now. He had the strongest feeling that things were about to get interesting.

18

That evening, Johnny went fishing again.

The high tide was in, the beach completely gone. He stood up by the fence above the high water mark, casting his rig out into the turbulent gray waters. The swells were coming in about every eight to nine seconds, cresting at well over six feet. The air was chill and damp. He used horse mullet again on an 18/0 leadered circle hook and cast it as far as he could out into the drink, nearly falling in more than once. A light wind was blowing with patchy squalls of rain.

He set up his Nikon on a tripod and rigged it with a remote shutter so one press of the button and the camera would capture whatever came out of the lower depths.

The waves kept bringing his rig back in.

It was frustrating.

Out over the sea in the distance he could see jagged bolts of cloud-to-water lightning. It was an impressive electrical show as it reflected off the columns of dark clouds and it was a good sign, he figured. He kept casting, hoping his bait might get sucked out far enough. About the time he was ready to call it a day, something started to happen. He felt that weird exhilaration and a seam of brilliant red unzipped the dark clouds over the Atlantic. He began to feel dizzy and woozy. He backed away from the edge of the breakwater so he did not accidentally fall in. It came quickly: the air grew thick and suffocating, unpleasantly hot. His scalp itched with prickly heat. He sweated, then shivered. He lowered himself to his knees until the worst of it passed.

When it had, the green sea opened up before him again.

It looked calm farther out, but as it neared the shore and came in contact with the modern world it grew agitated, the forces of the oncoming hurricane playing havoc with it. Huge rollers battered the breakwater, which was little more than an irregular shelf of rocks dumped there to stop erosion.

He stood up.

He clicked the shutter and got a few shots. The waves had brought his bait back in again. No matter, he cast it back out as far as he could. Just a little extinct fish, he thought, that's all I want. Just a nice hard piece of evidence no one can possibly dispute.

The line jerked.

Here we go.

The line jerked several more times and he could feel an impressive weight on the end of it. Whatever it was, it had securely hooked itself now. He played out some slack so his visitor would not get spooked. He moved up through the sand until he reached the road and crossed it. Then he locked down the reel and started playing with his trophy, give and take, give and take, tiring it, bringing it in a little closer each time. Whatever it was, it was heavy and it was unbelievably strong. When it ran he had all he could do to stay on his feet.

Finally, a good thirty minutes into it, he had it.

He began slowly, patiently reeling it in. He knew damn well there was no way he was going to drag whatever it was up over the rocks and sand to the side of the road where he wanted it. Just no way. This is where a helper would come in handy, he knew. Somebody to net the fish or drag it out of the water.

The idea of that made him laugh.

You didn't grab creatures from the Cretaceous sea and drag them out of the water; they grabbed *you* and dragged you into the water.

But all he wanted by that point was a good shot of it, nothing more. The trick would be to at least get it up onto the rocks for just a minute or so. Then he could get some decent pictures of it.

He kept reeling and reeling, landing whatever it was.

He only stopped once when some leviathan far beyond the cliffs themselves broke the surface, jumping up into the air and crashing back down in an explosion of white water. Whatever it was, it must have been immense.

"Don't worry about it," he said under his breath.

He could see a huge gray shape just beneath the water now about fifteen feet out. It rose and fell with the sucking action of the waves, which were working with him now—bringing his trophy in— rather than against him. He saw a perfectly ordinary, albeit large, tail fin break the surface. He had himself an ordinary, but hopefully extinct fishie.

The waves were pinning it against the rocks.

He had the sonofabitch.

Johnny thought: Next stop for you, Mr. Fish, is the cover of Nat Geo.

That was, *if* he could get it out of the water and it wasn't going to be easy. The damn thing had to be at least four feet long if not five. It was just waiting there, securely hooked. Shaking, Johnny took hold of the line and started pulling it in. Jesus, it weighed a ton. He pulled and pulled until a particularly ugly silvery fishy face was staring right at him. He clicked the shutter…and then it lunged. It shot right out of the water at him. He saw an immense mouth of sharp fanglike teeth that came within ten inches of his nose before dropping back into the water.

He saw his rod get yanked into the deeps.

Damn thing was making for the open ocean with his expensive rod and reel. There was no way in hell he was going in after it. When he caught his breath, he went over to the Nikon. He'd gotten a shot of it. Not a good one, but enough so that its bulging eyes and huge teeth could be seen.

As the Cretaceous sea faded away, he wondered with some amusement if his rod and reel would end up fossilized somewhere. Now wouldn't that be a trip?

19

"You think I'm crazy? You think I'm half out of my mind, right?"

Nate slowly dried glasses with a bar rag, one after the other, going out of his way to not make eye contact with Johnny. "No," he said. "Not saying you're crazy. Not saying anything at all."

Johnny licked his lips. They were dry. Too much time out in the wind and weather. His mouth seemed perpetually dehydrated, his skin always cold. After he got back from North Beach, he went right to the Blue Fin for a drink which became two, then three, and finally four. Somewhere during the process, he'd spilled everything to Nate. He told him the stories and showed him the pictures and although Nate was obviously astonished and disturbed by the images, he was not exactly surprised. What he wanted, Johnny knew, was to get the hell away from him but there were only four other people in the bar and he'd already refreshed their drinks. There was really nowhere for him to go.

"Say what's on your mind, Nate. You can't insult me. I've been worked on by experts. It rolls right off my back. Tell me what you think."

"I think you're going to get yourself killed."

"And?"

But Nate just shook his head. He was staring up at the plasma screen on the wall. The Weather

Channel was reporting on the hurricane nearly continuously. They had their usual assemblage of idiot meteorologists standing around with raincoats on, trying to speak above the moan of the wind. It hadn't hit Seagull like that yet, but by tomorrow night it would.

Through the wide bay windows of the Blue Fin, Johnny could see twilight suspended above the Atlantic out there. The wind was getting strong now and he could see big waves and whitecaps, streaks of gurgling foam.

"Nate?"

Nate was dissembling a pyramid of glasses behind the bar and packing them away in a wooden crate. Several windows of the restaurant had already been boarded over. Everyone on Seagull Island was battening down the hatches now, getting ready for the big blow...all except a particularly relentless and annoying man named Johnny Horowitz who was sitting on the doorstep of the biggest fucking story in human history.

"Nate," he said, pulling off his drink. "I get the feeling you're ignoring me."

Nate sighed. "Why don't you leave that business alone? Why risk your life, your sanity? Why, Johnny?"

"Money."

"Money?"

"Goddamn right, money. Think about it, my friend. People like dinosaurs. Fuck, they love 'em! It's not just the old scientists with long white beards fooling with fossil bones or kids playing with plastic T. Rexes anymore...now it's *everyone.* It's a pop cultural phenomena. Forget vampires and werewolves and all that old Bela Lugosi/Lon Chaney shit. Forget evil clowns and the walking dead and that Stephen King shit. That stuff is pedestrian. It's for the kiddies. People want monsters, Nate. Oh yes, they do, but they want *real* monsters, not make-believe boogeyman crap," Johnny said, catching sight of himself in the mirror behind the bar and realizing he was ranting. More so, he was obsessed and driven and near-fanatical like some street corner preacher on a milk crate prophesying doom and gloom. "They want horrors, they want beasts, they want *monsters* that have a scientific stamp of approval that gives them the sort of legitimacy all the possessed little girls, drunken zombies, and limp-wristed Transylvanian bloodsuckers will never know. They want giant man-eating fucking sharks and Jurassic Parks and drooling monsters out of time, beasts from 20,000 fathoms and giant behemoths and Godzillas even. Monsters, man, monsters...but *real* monsters, Nate. Things long extinct that maybe, possibly, *hopefully* have survived somehow into the modern age to terrify us and thrill us. They want mega-toothed primal visions, gigantic saurian horrors from the lost world, the skeletons that still tremble in the primordial closet of our race memory, and the shadows that stand *behind* the shadows cast over our earliest ancestors and the seed of all our collective terrors of the dark unknown ocean depths. They don't want fucking dragons, Nate, they want the *archetypes* of dragons. And somebody has to give that to them. Somebody has to offer that service and collect the fucking cash so Mr. and Mrs. Joe Blow Fucking Crow and the little squirts can look face-to-face with the meat-eating, bone-crunching monsters of prehistory and see how good they got it now, how safe and cozy things are…you dig?"

"Yeah, I dig, Johnny. Just take it easy."

Johnny laughed. "Take it easy, he says. *Nate,* out there at North Beach you've got the greatest cash cow in history just waiting to be fucking milked like a swollen tit. Pictures will be worth thousands. Videos worth millions. And to see them in the flesh or bring a living one back to some zoo? Fucking *hundreds of millions.* No, don't dismiss me as some city-bred urbane idiot even if that's exactly what I happen to be. Consider what I said. I can't do this alone."

Nate fixed him another Beefeater and tonic. "Drink that.   Drink it and forget about this nonsense."

Johnny just smiled. He couldn't seem to stop. There was nothing whimsical or cheerful about that smile; it was the smile of a skull. It was fixed and almost delirious. "C'mon, Nate. You don't think it's nonsense, now do you? I know you don't."

Nate didn't answer that. He just looked away.

Johnny wasn't going to give up that easy. Somebody on this goddamn rock was going to admit there were monsters out there. One way or another, they were going to.

He hadn't slept more than three hours a night since this all began.

How the hell could he? Christ, it was life-changing.

Night after night, he lay there, wondering if enormous, impossible beasts from the cellar of time were even then dancing around on the sands of North Beach. He fretted, hell, *worried* that he was missing out on something incredible. That was part of it. It made him toss and turn. But more than that, the adrenaline and possibility made his eyes refuse to shut. Adrenaline in that he had seen things nearly beyond human comprehension. And possibility in that the very existence of a Cretaceous Gateway opened up immense realms of wonder…and profit. Still photos would be worth a lot and videos would be nearly priceless, as he'd told Nate.

But why stop there?

How about television documentaries and books and lecture tours and guest appearances? Oh yeah, this was the real thing, baby. He could already smell all that green folding money. And, of course, there was scientific merit here, too. Those eggheads would be falling over themselves to study beasts that had been extinct for over 65,000,000 years.

And the great, truly unbelievable thing was that Johnny was the first on this one.

He was poised to become the fucking Steve Irwin of the Mesozoic…no, screw that, the Steve *Jobs* of the Cretaceous. So if he was a little on edge and dancing precariously on the hysterical tip of a pin, then so be it.

And what he needed to get the ball rolling was not still photos, but fucking video.

A video of the Cretaceous would make the Zapruder Film look like something off of *America's Funniest Home Videos.* Amusing, but inconclusive. What he was going to film would be the granddaddy of them all. The single most persuasive and shocking piece of film in the history of mankind.

The wheels in his head kept turning and they just wouldn't stop.

"Nate, just humor me a minute, okay?"

Nate sighed and put his hands flat on the bar top. "I'm listening."

"My guess is that North Beach is not for sale, am I right?"

He shook his head. "No, all beaches are public property. This is a tourist trap for godsake."

"Figured that. So chances are, the island fathers won't let me buy it."

"Probably not."

"But when they see the money I make off that particular piece of real estate, they are going to be all over it and you know it. I don't know what kind of ma-and-pa *Hee-Haw* collective operates Seagull—what do you have here? Town selectmen? City council? Three old hags scattering chicken bones and channeling the spirit of Mr. Green Jeans?—but there's no way in hell they'll let a guy like me run the show. They'll kick my ass right out the back door when they smell the money, but before they do I need to make my pile on this."

"It's your neck, Johnny. That's all I'm saying."

Oh, this guy was stoic, all right. What sort of grease was it going to take to get his gears moving? Johnny knew he needed another set of hands if he planned on landing something or getting a video of one of the big boys. It was too much for one man. He wanted Nate. He *needed* Nate.

"I'm willing to bet you don't make a bundle here, right? Enough to get by, but no serious cash. Am I right?"

Nate narrowed his eyes. "Yeah, not much."

"And you got kids, right?"

"Sure. They make life worth living."

"Cute as bunnies, I'd bet. A family guy like you, you could probably use some extra cash. Say a couple grand for a few hours of work?"

He had his attention now.

Johnny leaned over the bar. "I've got a little proposition for you, my friend."

20

Early the next morning before sunrise they drove out to North Beach in Nate's battered Ford pickup. They wanted to get out there for high tide because it would make what they wanted to do that much easier.

Hurricane Amelia was getting very close by then. A hurricane alert had been issued. Evacuation procedures were underway on the mainland. The last few boats were leaving Seagull Island. Johnny had convinced the owner of his hotel to let him weather it out down in the shelter in the basement. It wasn't cheap, but at least he'd have a hole to crawl into when the time came. The wind was kicking up to forty miles an hour by then and the rain was falling constantly, coming down in sporadic lashing sheets.

"Now that you're off work, Nate," Johnny said, "why don't you tell me about North Beach."

Nate just watched the snaking road. The sea was spraying over it now, drenching the truck with sudden gusts. He had to fight to keep it out of the ditch. "If you talked with Matt Packard, then you know all there is to know."

"Humor me." Johnny had his digital voice recorder running in his pocket just like he'd had that day at Packard's house. It was the juicy local stuff that would spice up his book—because somebody had to write the book, now didn't they? When this entire North Beach anomaly went viral and people began crowding to get a glimpse of the denizens of the deep, he would be there with the answers. His book would be a bestseller. In fact, he was quite certain it would top the New York Times bestsellers for months, if not a whole fucking year. Already he was imagining himself making the talk show circuit.

Nate talked in a low, tired voice almost as if he didn't want to be heard. He went over mostly things Packard had said. There were a few other items he recounted—missing kids, local folkore, gossip. Nothing exceptional save for a bit about an armed party of men that had descended on the place in the thirties.

"Matt didn't tell you about that?" Nate asked, genuinely surprised.

"No, not a thing. He was getting a little upset, though."

Nate shook his head. "I just know what my dad told me. Twenty, thirty guys went there with rifles and shotguns. They waited for the monster. They had dynamite. The monster never came. But it didn't matter, people around here knew the survivors of that beach party pretty damn well. They were all saying pretty much the same thing. People believed them then and they believe them now. You need proof of that, Johnny, North Beach being deserted day after day should convince you. Oh, the younger generations, they don't know about it. But Costello has the signs out there—riptides and all that—so they keep away. If they don't, he comes down hard on them."

"But you've never seen anything?"

"No. My mother didn't raise any fools. I knew enough to keep away."

Johnny smiled. "Well, today you'll see something. Something you'll never forget."

Nate pulled his truck to a stop before the fence. He just sat there, hands practically glued to the wheel.

"Let's do this," Johnny said.

21

The tide was coming in and the beach was under seven or eight feet of water that was wild and thrashing, throwing spouts fifteen feet in the air. The waves were cresting over ten feet, crashing into the breakwater rocks and flooding over them, washing right out into the road. The air was wet with driving rain and howling winds. It wasn't easy standing up in it and it was so loud they had to shout at each other to be heard.

"GOTTA…GOTTA BE BLOWING UP TO SIXTY MILES AN HOUR OR MORE!" Nate bellered, his face wet with rain. "THIS IS A WASTE OF TIME!"

Johnny braced himself against the truck. He could taste the sea on his lips. "JUST BE PATIENT! YOU'RE GETTING PAID!"

"NOT GETTING PAID TO DIE!"

They were both wearing hooded rain jackets and waterproof fisherman's bib pants, but still they were soaked to the skin in minutes.

The weather was absolutely chaotic, a real tempest coming in from the sea. And this was just the outer edge of Hurricane Amelia's wrath. When she came on for real, she would come on strong with winds of over a hundred miles an hour and sixteen foot waves that would crash against coastal buildings as the ocean flooded over the land. No man would be able to stand out in it. That was the sort of devastating fury that would peel off roofs, knock down trees, and turn houses into match sticks.

And it was coming, God yes, in only a few hours.

Johnny, trying to set an example of fortitude for Nate, pushed forward to where the fence had once been before the sea had knocked it down. The water was turbulent and violent and unbelievably loud. The crashing breakers sounded like explosions. Water drenched him, the wind hit him, the rain made it impossible to see. He was barely staying on his feet.

But I can't leave, he thought. I just can't. If that Cretaceous Gateway is ever going to be thrown wide it will be today. And if it opens, things are going to be seen and I want some shots of them. The storm will strand things and I'll be there to put them on ice. Goddamn, yes.

Nate shouted something to him and retreated back into the cab of the trunk. The wind was punching into it, making it shake on its springs. Johnny thought he was going to abandon him and drive off, but he just sat in there, staring out through the rain-beaded glass with taciturn eyes.

Johnny fought through the storm and got his hands on the truck.

It was good to feel something solid. Something he could grab onto if the wind decided to take him for a ride. It was a matter of waiting now. That was the worst part of it all. It was one thing when the weather was decent, but this was hell on Earth.

Finally, he gave up, climbing into the truck with Nate.

"You finally showing some good sense?"

Johnny shook his head, trying to massage some feeling back into his face. The pelting rain had made it go numb. "Let's just wait a little bit, okay? Give it fifteen or twenty minutes. If nothing happens, then we better head back. This is worse than I thought."

"North Beach is facing the blow," Nate told him. "If it wasn't for those high cliffs and those rock pilings diverting the storm a bit, it would have thrown both of us on our asses. And it's just getting going."

"Twenty minutes," Johnny said.

"Twenty. No more. After that, you can stay if you want, but I'm getting under cover. If you're smart—and that seems debatable—you'll come with me."

"I've got a berth over at the hotel."

"For an arm and a leg, I'll bet. You come home with me. My family will get a kick out of you, a first-class monster hunter."

Johnny sat there, shivering. The wind was howling like a freight train out there, the truck shaking like it was going to flip over at any moment. A month ago, he knew, he would have been scared shitless of a real monster of a hurricane like this, but now he just saw it as an inconvenience. Bad weather standing between him and a fortune.

The silence in the cab was oppressive, so Nate started chatting on about other hurricanes he'd been through and what he'd seen and felt, the destruction they left in their path. They were grim stories, but Nate was an islander and he knew in the final analysis that even if your house blew away and your place of business was crushed like a beer can and all that you owned was blown out into the Atlantic, as long as you and your family lived through it, it was all okay.

"In the end, Johnny," he said, "all that really matters is your loved ones, your family. You can make more money and start another business and build another house, but once you lose what you love best, once your heart is broken in pieces…well, you just can't get another now can you? Final is final."

Nate was good-hearted.

God, he was made of gold. A good father, a good friend. Loyal, trusting, exceptionally practical in all things. Johnny almost felt guilty dragging him into the middle of this whole mess. Maybe what he needed to do was to follow Nate's example and forget all about the Gateway and what it brought. There was trouble there and death. This was something he'd felt right from the start.

But you could retire, a greedy voice in his head told him. *Think about it. You could work this for all it's worth and when the story breaks, you'll have all your ducks in orderly rows and those duckies, my boy, they're going to be worth millions. This one thing can let you retire in style. Think about that. Just think about it.*

Yet, as he listened to Nate talk of his children and his hopes for their future, he wanted to kiss it all good-bye because it was trouble and he knew it was trouble. His life was synthetic and dirty and depthless. He had no family, no real friends, not even any damn kids.

"That's the great part about children, Johnny," Nate went on. "Even if you're a complete loser, they still think you're grand. Look at me? A bartender, an odd-job man, a sometimes fisherman and clam-digger, a part-time carpenter…God, I'm surely not much. I've got no millions. I've no great legacy to pass on. I've only got myself and you know what? To my young ones, that's more than enough. They still think I'm a king and smarter than any other ten men." Nate laughed. "Ha! They'll get older and realize their old man ain't so smart nor particularly special, but they'll still love me because they'll know I've done everything I can for them and loved them with all my heart."

The old Johnny had a strong desire to make some sarcastic, derisive comment. Nate and his soft soap and fuzzy memories and hearts full to bursting with love. Jesus. The old Johnny was too cynical to accept any of that. *Chicken Soup for the Islander's Soul.* That's all it was. He'd been in love before or, at least, he thought he had, but each and every time it fell apart. His chicken soup was always watery and hardly ever stuck to the ribs. Hell, most times its taste faded by morning.

That's what the old Johnny was thinking.

But the new Johnny kind of liked the sound of it. It made him laugh out loud. And not skeptically or acerbically, but with a warmth he felt flooding out from the core of his being. "Maybe I should forget about it," he said. "Maybe I should at that. Maybe I should quit taking pictures of people. Maybe I should come here and hang out with you, Nate, eh? Clambakes and odd-jobs and what-nots. A beach bum lifestyle."

"You should, Johnny. You might find yourself here. The sea can be a good teacher. It can show you what matters most."

It sure sounded good. Johnny had images of opening a pizza joint or something for the tourists— he was in possession of a highly-guarded, ultra-secret family thin crust recipe that belonged to a famous Brooklyn pizzeria that knocked people off their feet it was so good—and making a living. Sure, get a shack on the beach and sell pizza during the tourist season and read all those books he had boxed up but never got around to. Maybe he could start doing some watercolors again like when he was a teenager and doing a lot of fishing—before this little excursion into the unreal, he had never fished a day in his life. But he liked it. He damn well liked it. It was a great, satisfying way to spend a day just casting out into the surf. Sure, he could do that. It could have been a very good life.

But it wouldn't happen.

He knew it wouldn't happen.

He'd be fifty next year and he couldn't spend his declining years crawling through bushes and hiding under cars to get shots of celebrities. Hell, the next time Jean Claude Van Damme kicked him in the rocks his nuts just might not recover. They'd probably fly up into his head and bounce off the inside of his skull like pinballs. He liked the idea of being a beachcomber, but it was hardly realistic. When he was young, dreams like that made him walk on clouds for days. Now they just made him feel his years. He was too damn old to dream and fantasize. He needed to get out of the tabloid racket and there was only one way he was going to do that.

It was about that time that the truck stopped rocking.

It was still raining, but lightly.

"What the heck?" Nate said, after it had been quiet for over a minute. "Damn Amelia just blew over?"

But as soon as he unrolled his window, Johnny knew it wasn't that at all.

The Gateway was opening.

22

Nate stepped out of the truck and Johnny followed him. Behind them, the storm was still whipping across the island, but before them it had been neutralized for the most part. The sun had already risen in the modern world, but in the Cretaceous world it was just coming up far to the east, hazy and indistinct, a blood-red ball going to orange. The sea was crystal green—probably owing to plankton biomass enrichment which was well above current levels—and calm, a mist lifting off the surface, blowing landward in a heavy sea fog. The air was warm, heavy, and very moist. The closer to shore, the more the storm was felt, the waves cresting at eight or nine feet, but crashing much more gently.

Nate was down on his hands and knees, vomiting at the water's edge. He was overwhelmed by it all, but Johnny knew that it would pass. The transition was a little shocking the first few times, but when you knew what to expect it wasn't so bad.

Johnny stared out across the misty waters of time.

Huge puffy gray clouds scudded across the sky, the orange light of the rising sun reflecting against them and over the water. He heard a bird cry out and saw several pteradons wing gracefully out to sea, riding the breezes. It was a majestic sight. Their shrieking cries were not that much different than those of gulls, but louder, deeper, almost musical-sounding. It was a melody that had not been heard since the Cretaceous extinction 65,000,000 years before. It was haunting.

By this point, Nate was on his feet. "It's…it's beautiful," he said.

And it was. Pure nature: primal, wild, unsullied. A world before men dirtied the waters and fouled the air. About as close to natural perfection as you could get. Even the beautiful paintings of the Mesozoic that Johnny had seen on the internet could not do this primordial splendor justice. Yes, it was beautiful and like anything beautiful, it was also incredibly deadly. Where the sea met the sand was probably a very hazardous place in the ancient world. The scavengers would have come to feed on the rotting stranded organisms and the predators would have come to feed on them while immense marine reptiles would have waited under the waters to attack.

The rain was barely falling by then. It was more of a pervasive mist than anything else.

Johnny lit a cigarette and blew smoke into the wind. His mind was dreamy and distant and he could almost *feel* this place as if he had seen it before, a billion-billion lifetimes ago. Maybe his remote ancestors had scavenged a beach like this and their memories were locked in his genetic code. It all seemed so vaguely familiar and not because of his other experiences with the Gateway, but because of what was inside of him, what he felt reverberating from the very subcellar of ancestral memory. Even the smell of the Cretaceous dawn filled him with the most alarming sense of déjà vu.

"My God," Nate said. "It…it takes your breath away."

"Do you see now, Nate? Do you see how important this all is?"

"Yes. It's incredible."

Johnny smiled. Nate was smiling, too. There was a goofy, almost soporific grin on his face and his eyes had a funny hypnotic glaze to them. He looked stoned, light-headed, wistful. He was mainlining on all that he saw and all that he felt and there was no drug that could match it. He, like Johnny himself, was an addict. He could have stood there like that for hours and watched, just watched, the primordial perfection of a world long dead suddenly come vibrantly alive.

"All right," Johnny said. "Now you see and now you know. We better get down to business."

"Yeah…okay."

Nate was too transfixed by it all to realize the danger they were in. Johnny had to give him a little push to get him working again. When he finally moved, he blinked his eyes a couple times, and said, "Wow." Together they got the equipment out of the back of the truck and got down to work. The Gateway would only stay open for so long. Today, because of the hurricane and its assorted electrical and magnetic disturbances, it would probably stay open longer, but there was a limit. Johnny did not know what it was, but he was certain there had to be an outer limit.

They had about two-hundred feet of dog chain. The good stuff that was used to restrain pit bulls and other fighting dogs. They had hooked an 8" shark gaff to it and impaled a three pound rump roast on the barb. They attached this to a Redi-Rig shark float that would dangle it out in the deep water where they hoped they'd bring in something no one would ever believe.

"Let me do this," Nate said.

He took the meat hook and about five feet of chain as Johnny stood back—*way* back—and went at it like an Olympian, swinging the roast around and around like he was competing in the hammer throw, gathering centrifugal force and then tossing it with incredible velocity. The meat went out well over a hundred feet, right over the tops of the tallest waves that would have washed it back in.

"Very nice," Johnny said.

"I used to compete a long time ago."

They stared out at the lozenge-shaped white float with its red stripes. It was well past the gray, modern waters and well into the green Cretaceous depths. Johnny had no idea how deep it might have been out there at high tide. Realistically, eight or nine feet during normal high tide, but with Amelia probably deeper. And perhaps deeper still as it intersected the Cretaceous sea.

"Now we just wait."

Nate was okay with that. He leaned up against the truck, marveling at all he saw, while Johnny moved about taking shots of birds and breaching fish, several long necks that broke the surface and disappeared as quickly. It was a waiting game and while Nate was very calm about it all, Johnny was nervous as hell. Nervous because he wanted a physical specimen—there could be no denying the carcass of an ancient marine creature—and nervous because when the Gateway closed, they were going to be in the teeth of a hurricane nearing full force.

The float was nudged.

"Hey! Look there!" Nate said.

Johnny was looking, all right. The float bumped around in the water as if something below were nudging it, perhaps nibbling on it but refusing to bite just yet. He and Nate took hold of the chain, taking up some of the slack. They wanted to see the float get yanked below the surface and then they were going to hook their beasty. The float kept bumping around and they saw the silvery body of a large fish break the surface. It went on that way for maybe five minutes and then the water exploded and the float went under.

"Shit," Johnny said.

They took up the slack and gave the chain a good yank with everything they had, hopefully setting the hook. There was something on the other end and they could feel it snapping at the bait. They had it. They pulled and it pulled. It was very strong. They kept well away from the water's edge so it did not pull them in. When it pulled hard, they gave it slack; when it stopped moving, they started yanking on it. They were both nervous as hell by that point. They still had no idea what it was. There was only a large black shape that the glare of the ancient sun on the water stopped them from seeing in any detail.

But it was big. Hell, it was *very* big.

They played tug of war with it another fifteen minutes, both of them sweating and panting by then. It was strong, damned strong. But they both knew that huge sharks had been landed by simply tiring them out in just this fashion.

"I think it's starting to come in," Nate said.

The shadow under the water was getting closer, but it was still out sixty feet or so. But gradually, yes, it was coming in closer. It wasn't trying to run anymore. Johnny was getting very excited. Once they got it in close, they would tie off the chain to the trailer hitch on the back of the pickup and drag it up out of the depths. It was going to work, it was really by God going to work.

"All right, Mr. Prehistoric Fish," Nate said, "we gonna bring you in nice and slow, real gentle-like...and easy...that's it...that's it...no need to fight your friends. We just want a good look at you."

The shadow was forty feet out now and still coming, Nate cooing to it, talking to it, trying to calm it with a nonstop monologue of sweet nothings. It was coming closer, foot by foot. By that point, Johnny was shaking, absolutely shaking.

"Johnny," Nate said, "our old friend he just wants to come in sweet and easy. He don't want to fight no more. Hook that chain to the hitch. Go on, do it."

With trembling fingers, Johnny did just that, coiling it around the hitch and through the bumper and securing it to itself with the heavy duty snap hook at the end. He pulled on it. It was secure and strong. He started up the truck in the gloom and rain and pulled it across the road so the hitch was pointing out to sea. He climbed out and went over to Nate who was still playing his fish, talking to it and drawing it in link by link. It was about thirty feet out by then.

"She ain't no fish," he said, breathing in and out very fast now, his nerves near the breaking point. "Don't know what…but that ain't no fish."

Johnny saw a suggestion of a long, streamlined creature. A huge whalelike flipper that was black and leathery-looking broke the surface, moving with a very gentle stroking motion before going back under. High overhead, as if sensing what was going on below, pterosaurs were circling like buzzards. One of them dipped down over the water about twenty yards out and its wingspan was nearly that of a small plane. The wind it created smelled of brine and dead fish.

Johnny reached down for the chain.

He heard Nate grunt as if he had been kicked.

The creature had run again and with the chain taut in his grip, Nate was yanked off his feet and went airborne, flipping end over end and splashing down about fifteen feet out. An ice-cold terror rushing through Johnny, he dashed to the water's edge, nearly falling in himself. The waves crashed, throwing water in his face. "NATE! NATE!

NATE!" he called out, his voice echoing out across the sea.

Nate surfaced, gasping for breath and spitting out a column of water, his eyes bulging and his mouth hooked in a grimace of absolute fright. He started swimming towards the breakwater, doing the crawl, gasping and grunting with the exertion. He was pouring everything he had into it.

"SWIM!" Johnny called out to him, reaching for him with an outstretched hand. "SWIM! SWIM! FOR GODSAKE, SWIM!"

He was closer, the waves pushing him forward then tugging him backwards again. But he was mere feet from the breakwater. His fingertips brushed Johnny's own and then the suction of a wave pulled him back out again and he fought even harder to close the gap. And out there, maybe twenty feet from him, Johnny saw a huge dark form moving in his direction.

Then Nate was clinging to the breakwater, pulling himself up and Johnny had one of his hands. It was going to be okay. It was really going to be okay. And then—

It happened fast.

That shape out there came shooting forward like a rocket, riding just behind one of the big waves. It came vaulting out of the water and Johnny saw a huge maw like that of a crocodile lined with teeth like steak knives snap shut around Nate's midsection. It closed with incredible force and Nate let out one wet, rending, hysterical scream and Johnny heard bones snapping like twigs just as a spray of blood splashed into his face. The creature looked like a crocodile with huge flippers, its flesh reticulated with dark green bands against a dull yellow background. The force of it exploding from the surf threw Johnny back four feet or it might have had him, too. It flipped backwards with an amazing athletic grace, showing its near-phosphorescent white underbelly. Nate looked like a minnow in the jaws of a salmon. It dove back into the deeps with him.

Johnny clearly saw the hook impaled in its lower jaw.

Then…it was gone.

Hysterical, drenched with Nate's blood, he began to scream.

23

The chain was going back out, taking up all the slack they had pulled in. It made the sound a dog's chain will when a German Shepherd runs at full tilt. Then it snapped tight, the pick-up rocking on its frame. The beast was at least twenty feet long and God only knew how heavy. It pulled at the chain and the truck skidded about two feet over the road.

Johnny crawled away.

The fog had thickened by then and he could only see about twenty or thirty feet at most. The chain ran out from the back of the pickup, over the breakwater, and disappeared into the water right at the edge of the fog. As Johnny watched, it whipped back and forth violently as if the creature was trying to throw the hook and it probably was. The truck scraped over the road, shaking and trembling, bits of rusty metal dropping from its underside. Either the chain would break or the creature would throw the hook.

Johnny had seen that Cretaceous monster close-up and personal.

Something like it would not give up or give in.

It would worry itself right to death if it had to.

For the first time since any of this had started, Johnny was wishing like hell that the Gateway would just close already. He'd seen enough. He'd been through enough. And Nate was dead. *Nate was fucking dead.* And how was he supposed to explain any of it to the man's family? How could he tell Nate's wife and children that her husband and their doting, loving farther had just been gobbled up by a fucking Mesozoic sea monster? Nate…oh God…he had nearly begged Johnny to let it go, to leave it all alone, but he hadn't. He told himself he couldn't, but that was just greed talking. Greed and animal materialism demanding that he get more, more, more.

The truck jerked and bumped a few feet across the road.

How strong was that dog chain anyway and why didn't that goddamn Gateway close already? Why didn't it slam shut like door? Wasn't enough damage done?

Sure, he thought as he crouched there by the sand, the rain falling and the wind whistling out behind him, the crotch of his bib pants warm from his own piss. *Sure, enough damage has been done and you're the fucking cause of it. You couldn't back away, you couldn't leave well enough alone. Now a man—a good, decent man—is dead and you have no idea what you might have set into motion here.*

As the chain kept snapping and the truck slid closer to the water's edge, Johnny crept away on his hands and knees. He did not even feel like he was enough of a man to stand erect and walk. He was beaten down, slinking, less than human. He would have to get back to town, he would have to find Costello and tell him of the awful thing that had happened.

That was the only logical thing to do.

And then he heard a cry coming from the sea, a bellowing, deep, and resonant roar that sounded like a distant foghorn...only louder, more primeval and menacing, the guttural shriek of some prehistoric beast breaching from an ancient lake. It echoed out from the mist and Johnny felt himself go cold, then hot as it cut through the air. Sea birds out on the rocks dove in terror. The cry came again and it was louder and much closer. Pterosaurs scattered from the high cliffs.

He could feel something building in the air and he acquainted it with raw, unreasoning, primal terror. It was as if the Cretaceous world was holding its breath out of complete fear. He was shaking, sweating, his teeth chattering. He remembered very well the story that Matt Packard had told him, about the immense thing that came out of the sea. He knew he had to get out of there, but he didn't dare move. He huddled in the sand as if he was almost instinctively trying to make himself a smaller target. He felt like a rabbit with a hawk circling overhead. The terror started at the tips of his toes and went right up to the top of his head.

The cry came again and it was so close now it seemed to rattle his bones.

Packard had mentioned the awful smell of the thing, like canneries and fishing nets, but it was one thing to hear about it and quite another to smell it and Johnny *did* smell it. It came rolling in with the fog, hot and noxious and just sickening. It was the stink of sunken ships draped in green weeds, dredged sea bottoms and stagnant tidal pools, mountains of rotting kelp and the black seething mud of the abyss—warm and organic and moist, the smell of the creature he now saw coming through the fog. It was black and shiny like sealskin, its body streamlined and muscular and longer than two tanker trucks parked end to end. Its neck was bigger around than an old oak tree, its crocodilian head rising up over forty feet just as Packard had said. The sunlight gleamed off its immense teeth which jutted from the jaws like stalactites and stalagmites.

It opened its mouth and roared again and the world shook.

It dipped its immense head down into the water and seized something, chomping on it and swallowing it with a few biting gulps. It was the creature that got Nate. That horror had been at least twenty feet long and it looked like a mudskipper in the beak of a tern.

That more than anything gave Johnny a good idea of the scale of the thing. It was a fucking behemoth, an immense sea monster that science had probably never described. An absolute horror recalled only through the most distant echoes of race memory and rechanneled into sea serpents and dragons. This was the seed. Johnny was struck speechless by it. For a few moments, he did not even breathe.

Then it roared with absolute primal wrath and he started running.

He made it maybe a city block down the road before he felt the force of Hurricane Amelia. The winds knocked him off his feet as immense waves crashed landward and drenched him. Trees were bending and debris flying, wet sand and mud and stones pelting him. The rain was coming down so hard he couldn't see anything. When he squinted his eyes, the world was just a gray, raging chaos, the sea beyond foaming and erupting with spouts and gigantic waves. He knew his only chance was to reach Matt Packard's place. It wasn't far, but in this blow it might as well have been ten miles.

Still, he had no choice.

There was no other shelter.

He heard the beast roar again, but it sounded distant now as if it had gone back out to sea. Maybe the Gateway was closing. He could only hope it was, because the last time the creature had come ashore it had demanded an awful sacrifice.

24

It took him over an hour to make it to Seal City.

It was only a half a mile away but the rain was coming down in whipping gray sheets and the wind kept knocking him off his feet. Even leaning into it was no good. He had to crawl on all fours through the mud and water. Trees were down and hillsides were great gurgling mud slides. He tried to stay to higher ground because it was flooded everywhere. Power lines and their attendant poles were ripped right from the earth, some snapped literally in half. He saw cottages that had been stripped from their foundations. Out to sea in the distance, he saw the broken, overturned hulks of boats being battered by immense waves. Thunder rumbled and lightning flashed. The world was chaotic, cracking, blowing and screeching.

When he finally reached Seal City, he could barely see anything. Huge waves were coming inland, cresting over the docks and piers. Fish huts and little houses had been stripped away or shattered into kindling. Much of the roof had been stripped off the old cannery and huge, sucking whirlpools of gray water surged in the narrow streets amongst the houses.

By that point, Johnny had to nearly hug the ground to make it out to Matt Packard's cottage which, amazingly, still stood despite the fact that it was at ground zero of Amelia. It was on higher ground than the others, so it wasn't flooded out, but at the same time only put it directly in the monstrous path of the hurricane. How he made it out there to the cottage, he wasn't even sure, but by the time he beat on the door he could barely see anymore from the water spraying continually into his eyes. They felt swollen in their sockets, burning from the salt.

"MATT!" he cried. "MATT! DEAR GOD LET ME IN! PLEASE LET ME IN!"

But it was so damn loud out, he rather doubted he would be heard and he wasn't. He beat on the door on his hands and knees, the tempest raging around him. For all he knew Matt was calling to him, but with the constant thundering cacophony of the storm it was really hard to tell. Johnny felt beaten and weak, his face numb and his ears ringing. He would die out here. Yes, right on Matt Packard's stoop and after all he had been through, it didn't sound so bad. The very idea of closing his eyes was all that seemed to matter.

Then he heard something.

He thought it was Matt crying out to him, but when it came again, this time much louder, he knew it wasn't anything coming from inside the cottage but a foghorn-like primeval roaring coming from out to sea, cycling from the very guts of the hurricane. It was the cry of the beast and it was getting louder and louder, almost hysterical sounding, cutting right through the rumbling of the storm and the howling of the wind.

Johnny, his heart beating again, crawled along the front of Matt Packard's house, and peered out into the cyclone. The rain struck his face like hundreds of sharp little needles, but by that point he could barely feel any of it. The wind punched into him with incredible force and he had to cling to the cottage so he wasn't stripped away and tossed out into the maelstrom.

He heard the roar of the beast again.

Then he saw it.

He saw it rise from the ocean, leviathan and behemoth, a giant of the ages coming inland as it probably had during the Cretaceous, partly out of hunger and partly out of curiosity, but mostly out of the need to destroy and dominate. It passed right by the lighthouse on the farthest cay—Old Bristly—as it waded in, splashing through immense gurgling tidal pools that would have drowned a man but to it were mere puddles.

Then it turned.

It brought its head down low on its glistening elephantine neck in a straight horizontal line from its body. It eyed the lighthouse warily as if it were a rival. Its mouth pulled back from long interlocking teeth that looked like white icicles. It moved in closer to the light on its short, stout legs. It lifted up one enormous flipperlike foot, much like a cat preparing to stalk. Its entire body seemed to shudder, the musculature beneath the black-green skin rippling.

Then it lunged.

Underwater, it must have been a study in reptilian speed and fishlike grace, but on land it was somewhat clumsy as if its own gargantuan strength betrayed it. In the depths, it would have attacked the lighthouse with darting, lightning-quick agility, tearing it from its foundation in the blink of an eye, but without the stabilizing pressures of the depths to equalize it when it lunged, its entire massive weight went airborne and struck the lighthouse dead on.

The result was instantaneous.

The Bristol Point Light had withstood the onslaught of foul weather, battering waves, and tropical cyclones for nearly a century-and-a-half, but it was not made to withstand the dead weight of over eighty tons striking it broadside. The beast hit it and the tower collapsed, coming apart like a house of cards with a great rumbling crash.

Clinging to the edge of Matt Packard's resilient little dwelling, Johnny recalled watching a movie when he was a boy wherein a great dinosaurlike sea monster knocked down a lighthouse. For weeks and perhaps months afterward, particularly on nights when the rain and wind picked up, he feared the monster would come and knock his house down.

Silly, childish fears.

Except…now it was very close to becoming a reality.

The beast tore apart what remained of Old Bristly, scattering its bricks like dice with mighty sweeping motions of its tail. Its head darted about, striking like a cobra, tearing apart the carcass of the light and tossing things into the sea with violent shakes of its head—a railing, part of the oval roof, a section of the spiral staircase, and what looked to be the crystal mass of the light itself.

It had attacked Old Bristly as if for no other reason than the fact that the light offended it.

And maybe it had at that as the entire modern world would have offended it.

Lastly, the tower destroyed, pieces of it being tossed about by the wind and waves, the beast raised its neck up straight as a post and its jaws opened to expel a roar that sounded like it could have split mountains and laid forests flat.

But it was hardly done, its rage barely spent.

It was still coming in, moving even faster now despite the ninety-mile-an-hour winds that buffeted it and the thirty foot waves that broke against its oily hide. It moved from cay to cay until it zeroed in on the clustered fisherman's shacks of Seal City. It came out of the surf with an explosion of foam, casting a tidal wave before it that stripped away porches and overturned cars.

Johnny waited, stunned and motionless, the dizzying size of the thing taking his breath away. And on it came.

Boom, boom, boom.

Then, without further ado, it began to destroy the village.

25

By then, he was frantic and hysterical.

He beat on Matt's front door with his fists, his body. He kicked it. He bounced his head off of it. "MATT! MATT! MATT! JESUS H. CHRIST, LET ME IN! LET ME IN!" his voice shrieked. "OPEN THE DOOR, MATT! IT'S COME OUT OF THE FUCKING SEA! *IT'S COMING FOR ME!*"

Finally, the door opened a crack and the old man peered out suspiciously. "HELL YOU DOING OUT THERE IN THAT BLOW?" he called above the fury of the storm. He looked like he was going to say something else, too, but then he heard what Johnny had been hearing: the titanic roar of the creature.

And the sound of its feet: *Boom, boom, boom.*

It gave him pause, but no more. "HELL YOU DOING OUT THERE?" he shouted and it had to be the most absurd question that Johnny had ever heard. The beast was roaring and the hurricane was howling and Johnny was seconds away from shitting himself.

"LET ME IN!" he cried. "LET ME IN FOR GODSAKE!"

Packard backed his chair away from the door and Johnny pulled himself through, shaking like a wet dog. He bolted and secured the door, then followed his host back into the crowded living room where candles were flickering. All the windows of the house were set with heavy shutters against the storm so there was no way Packard had seen what was going on out there.

"You sure wait until the last minute," the old man said. "Any fool with a lick of common sense would have gotten himself to shelter hours ago. You're lucky to be alive."

"Sure," Johnny said.

Even with door closed, the windows shuttered, and the walls of stone, they still had to talk loudly. The storm sounded like a Boeing 707 passing overhead.

Johnny—dripping, traumatized, and speechless—just stood there in his wet things, staring at his host. *He must not know. He must not realize what's going on out there. He has no idea.*

"Power's out," Packard said. "Lot of racket out there. You're lucky I heard you at all. My hearing aid's been acting up all day."

There was a sudden concussion that shook the house. The walls rang out like tuning forks. It sounded like a tractor-trailer had been dumped from the sky out there.

Johnny swallowed. "It's back," he said. "It's come back out of the sea."

Packard smiled thinly. "Of course it has. It was bound to come sooner or later. I been waiting for it since I was twelve and now the day has come."

He knew.

He actually knew.

"It's gigantic...it's the biggest thing in...in...in..."

"In Creation, Johnny? Oh yes. If it's not, it'll do, I guess. It'll certainly do."

Johnny swallowed. "But you're just waiting here. You can't just sit here like this."

Packard laughed. "And why can't I? What would you have me do? Wheel myself into town? Surf to the mainland?" He patted his wheelchair. "For some of us, friend, there ain't nothing left to do but sit and wait and watch."

As the house trembled with what felt like seismic shockwaves, Johnny fell to his knees next to the old man's chair. He shook, he sobbed, he moaned deep in his throat. He dug a plastic Ziploc bag from inside his rain jacket. His cigarettes and lighter were in there along with his cash, credit cards, and ID.

His fingers trembling badly, he pulled on the cigarette until his mind cleared somewhat. "Nate's dead," he finally said. "He died right in front of me."

For the first time, Packard seemed concerned. His eyes narrowed in his craggy face. "Tell me."

So Johnny did. It didn't take very long.

"You just couldn't leave it alone, could you?"

Johnny wearily shook his head.

"Gonna be hard now for his kin. Real hard. You owe them, you know. Nate was a good boy and you owe his family. You have an obligation to them."

Johnny knew that he did. He told the old man he would take care of them and it wasn't some idle promise. Maybe he wasn't exactly a good person and had never been much with responsibilities, but down deep—*very deep*—he knew there was something good in him, something decent. If there was a way, he would take care of Nate's family. Hell, even if there *wasn't* a way, he'd take of them. He knew he would. He knew he had to. That was, if he could survive this…something which didn't look very hopeful at the moment.

"Help me up to the window, boy," Packard said. I gotta see it. One last time, I gotta see it."

It was insane under the circumstances…but Johnny understood that kind of insanity, that sort of compulsion. He had had to see, too, at North Beach again and again. He knew he couldn't talk the old man out of it any more than Nate had talked him out of it. There were times when common sense simply made no sense and this was one of them.

Packard didn't weight much.

Johnny boosted him up to the windowsill and he hung on with his arms. The glass on all the windows had been removed and replaced with heavy storm shutters. Johnny pulled the pins and undid the latches that held them in place and the wind did the rest. There was a creaking and the shutter went flying off into the storm as if it had been blown with a breaching charge.

And Hurricane Amelia came right in.

Wind and rain funneled through the window in a tempest. Johnny was instantly knocked on his ass, but Packard hung onto the sill. Despite his age, his arms were like iron from doing the work of arms *and* legs. Books and bottles flew from shelves, papers and photographs and anything that wasn't tied down went spinning in a wild whirlwind. Paintings were peeled from the walls, chairs upended, and beer cans sent into orbit.

Yet, through it all, the old man hung on.

Johnny doubted that even the beast could have pulled him free.

The storm was loud, but not quite loud enough to muffle the screaming of the village fishermen and their families. Johnny forced himself to the window and braced himself there as the house seemed to vibrate in the blow.

What he saw was unbelievable.

It was like watching Godzilla stomp Tokyo.

The beast was roaring and bellowing, worked up into an absolute frenzy of destruction. It smashed houses like eggshells. It stomped them with its great feet and scattered them with its snaking tail. Its massive jaws peeled roofs free and it butted down walls with the battering ram of its head. It plucked people from the ruins, biting them in half and swallowing them without so much as chewing. It went after them like an aardvark sorting through an ant hill.

"IT'S KILLING THEM!" Johnny shouted. "IT'S KILLING THEM ALL!"

"YES! YES!" Packard shouted back at him. "I TOLD THEM! I WARNED THEM IT WOULD COME BACK BUT THEY WOULDN'T LISTEN! I WAS A CRAZY SENILE OLD COOT! NOW THEY KNOW! GOD HELP THEM, NOW THEY KNOW!"

The beast turned, perhaps realizing that it had left one dwelling untouched.

It began to come towards the cottage with thundering elemental wrath. Johnny doubted whether there was anything short of an A-bomb that could have stopped it. It plowed through the ruins of Seal City, bearing down on the cottage, lifting its huge feet and sending them crashing down again. Closer and closer. As it moved, its tail swung and its head went from side to side. It was on land, but that was probably how it moved in the Cretaceous sea.

Boom, boom, boom.

The closer it got, he could see that its streamlined flippers were really not flippers at all but long, scythe-shaped paws, the toes webbed with membranous fans of tissue. Their black gleaming claws tore into the earth and propelled the creature ever forward.

Boom, boom, boom.

It seemed to be moving faster now, water and mist and debris flying all around it. Johnny saw its flat yellow eyes that had to be the size of car tires, the huge spikelike teeth that jutted from its mouth even when it was closed. Nothing could stop it as it zeroed in on the cottage, the earth shaking from its stride.

BOOM, BOOM, BOOM!

It was so close by then that Johnny could smell its hide which was like a truckload of dead fish at first and then a musky, oily odor of snakeskins. He tried to pry Packard away from the window, but he shrugged him off. This was it. This was what he had been waiting for since he was twelve years old. Nothing would stop him from looking death in the eye, absolutely nothing. This was how he *wanted* to die. Not sick and old and infirm in bed, but like this. He wanted his life to have a grand, dramatic climax and his wish was about to be granted.

The beast was at the cottage now.

From his position on the floor, gagging on the awful smell of the creature, Johnny could see the elongated fishlike scales of its gleaming skin, the vibrant shine of them, electric green darkening into abyssal black. It filled the window and the old man was calling to it like it was a lost puppy he had not seen since childhood, an old and valued friend. The beast, its colossal snout within feet of Packard, appraised him with its baleful yellow eyes. Slime dripped from its jaws. Its nostrils flared as it breathed. Slowly, its jaws opened to reveal the dark tongue and pink mouth, teeth like stabbing swords.

Packard said something.

The beast growled at him with an exhalation of hot, fetid breath that blew his hair back from his head. If Johnny hadn't have known better, he would have thought they were in some sort of communication, that an understanding had been reached and the beast was now going to keep its part of the bargain. Its jaws yawned wide and it struck. It collapsed the wall around the window and seized Packard, teeth impaling him like spikes. He shrieked and blood jetted from his mouth, becoming a fine mist that blew through the air. Johnny felt it break wetly against his face. The old man was drawn into its mouth and that was the last Johnny saw of him, then the beast, jaws closed and bloodstained, smashed its head into the cottage and the entire thing came apart like it was built of sticks.

Johnny cried out and covered his head.

The last thing he saw were immense cracks fanning through the stone walls and then the cottage came down on top of him.

26

It was much later when he woke.

It was very dim and he knew it had to be near dark. He moved one arm, then another. They were free. He moved his legs. Other than bumping his knee into something, they were free, too. He tried to move his body. It moved. He was not pinned or crushed. He was bruised and banged up, aching and godawful thirsty, but he was still whole and still alive.

Now he needed to get out if that was possible.

He tried to move forward, but he ran into part of a wall, so he scooted on his ass, feet-first. He was moving. As luck or fate or God himself would have it, he was in some kind of tunnel whose walls were timbers and stone and assorted rubble. He kept moving inch by inch until he knew he was close because he could smell the brine of the sea.

Just go easy, he told himself. There's no hurry.

And there wasn't. He was certain of it. He could not hear the storm anymore which meant the worst of it had blown itself out. That was something. As he squirmed his way free, he tried not to think of Nate or Matt or anyone else. There was only survival now and he was accepting of this. Later, there would be time for guilt, self-recrimination, and self-loathing; now escape was all there was.

It took him fifteen or twenty minutes to wriggle his way free of the wreckage and then he pushed himself outside, landing in a pool of standing water. He stood up uneasily on tottering legs. It was about an hour before sundown, he figured. The wind had died down now to an ordinary sea breeze. Huge masses of white clouds were piled up in the sky. It was warm and humid.

Around him, was devastation.

The village was destroyed. The beast had decided to retreat back into the sea right through the old cannery which was nearly entirely collapsed. It looked like the world's largest bonfire waiting for a match, just a towering heap of planks and timbers and logs.

Johnny dug his cigarettes from the Ziploc bag inside his coat and smoked as he viewed the wreckage. His digital camera was gone along with his pictures, save the ones Janet had. Nobody in their right mind was going to believe that a sea monster did this. The idea was laughable. In fact, Johnny started giggling. His life had become something from the *Weekly World News* or *Fate* magazine. If he told his tale, people would laugh at him. There were the pictures that Janet had…but that's all there was.

"And that, folks," he said under his breath, "is the end of the goose and the golden eggs."

He stepped around puddles and bricks and debris.

His foot slipped and he fell into a pool of…something. It was black and steaming and vile-smelling. Jesus. He climbed his way out, trying brush the stuff free. It was tarry and greasy.

Shit.

That's the word that popped into his head. It was shit, as in feces. The awful ammonia stink of it made his eyes water and his stomach flip over itself. It was a pile of shit. Sea monster shit. That fucking beast had taken a major code brown dump about the size of a backyard pool and he had waltzed right into it. Dipped in it, waded in it, swam in it. It was incredible and humiliating and very funny.

That fucking behemoth blew mud and I stepped into it. Fucking thing pinched a loaf and dropped a deuce, it launched an ass rocket and squeezed out a Cleveland goddamn steamer…and I took a dive right in it. Dipped in shit, I am.

There was poetic justice in that, he supposed, karmic retribution and all that, but he could not bring himself to think about it. In the end, he was just as big of a fool as he'd always suspected he was. Alec Baldwin was proven fucking right: he *was* a shit-crawling worm. There was something very liberating about accepting one's true nature.

When Costello made it out there just before sunset in an SUV, he found Johnny sitting on the wreckage that had been Matt Packard's house, smoking a cigarette and staring into a giant pool of foul brown seepage. He was filthy. He looked like a coal miner after a hard day in the shafts.

"Mr. Horowitz?" Costello said. "Are you all right?"

"Do I look all right?"

Costello's partner—a young cop with freckles on his face—looked around at the ravaged village, the debris and mud and smashed cannery, the pile of rubble that marked Old Bristly in the distance. "God, it wiped out everything. *Everything.*"

"Yes, it did," Johnny said.

He just kept shaking his head. "A hurricane….a hurricane did all this?"

Johnny laughed dryly. "Of course it was a hurricane…what do you think it was? A giant fucking monster from the sea?"

✦THE END✦

Made in the USA
Lexington, KY
04 July 2014